Cambridge

Cambridge

A NOVEL BY
Caryl Phillips

ALFRED A. KNOPF   NEW YORK
1992

THIS IS A BORZOI BOOK
PUBLISHED BY ALFRED A. KNOPF, INC.

Copyright © 1991 by Caryl Phillips
All rights reserved under International and Pan-American
Copyright Conventions.
Published in the United States by Alfred A. Knopf, Inc.,
New York. Distributed by Random House, Inc., New York.
Originally published in Great Britain by Bloomsbury Publishing
Ltd., London.

Library of Congress Cataloging-in-Publication Data

Phillips, Caryl.
Cambridge: a novel / by Caryl Phillips. — 1st American ed.
p. cm.
ISBN 0-679-40532-1
I. Title
PR9275.S263 P4727   1992
823'.914—dc20   91-53127
                                                         CIP

Manufactured in the United States of America
Published February 5, 1992
Reprinted Once
Third Printing, March 1992

For Elizabeth

Prologue

England.

The ship was ready to sail. She remembered.

A tall carriage drawn by a pair of horses bedecked with shiny harnesses. Father returned. What now? And daughters sacrificed to strangers. A woman might play upon a delicate keyboard, paint water-colours, or sing. Her father conducted himself as a stern audience. He stood before her, his legs slightly apart, his hands clasped behind his back. She sat upright, her hands knitted together in her lap. A woman must run the household, do the accounts, command the domestic servants, organize the entertaining, but her relations with her children were to be more formal. (Hence the governess and the nursemaid.) She remembered her mother, who had died when she was a young girl. Her mind carried a vignette of her mother in her matutinal pose upon the *chaise-longue*. It seemed so long ago now. It must be difficult for Papa to understand the heart of a woman without the refining influence of a wife. Papa's decision was that she should travel to his West Indian estate and on her return marry Thomas Lockwood (who was ably provided for). She looked into her father's eyes and thought she saw his pity for the daughter who was being offered a fifty-year-old widower with three children as a mode of transportation through life. She spoke no words. She locked eyes with him, as though to drop her gaze would be to end the years of painful communication they had sought to construct. Still she spoke no words. Papa, I have buried feelings. She listened as her voice unspooled in silence. Feelings locked deep inside of me, hopes that demand that I must not abandon them for years of cold fleshiness made intimate only by the occasional brushing of lips against cheek. Do you understand? He gazed imperiously at his daughter. She saw now the determination to insure his own future. Lowering her eyes she fell into a gloomy study. The rude mechanics of horse-trading. She had once overheard her father insisting that sensible men should only trifle with these children of a larger growth. And then he laughed. To reside under the auspices of a 'petticoat government'! But she had never doubted that Papa loved her. That evening he planted a light kiss upon her forehead. For a few moments it began to live a life of its own. Then, as ever, it faded. And now she simply waited for the ship to haul anchor. The truth was she was fleeing the lonely regime which fastened her into backboards, corsets and stays to improve her posture. The same friendless regime which advertised her as an ambassadress of grace. Almost thirty. Too old to be secretly stifling her misery into lace handkerchiefs.

The ship was ready to sail. She remembered.

England.

The truth.

I

We are now on board and can truly claim to be a part of this wooden society. Isabella and I are heavily fatigued but worse than this we cannot but be appalled by the condition of what will pass for our home during the weeks ahead. In short, the cabin is in a state of disrepair. This is a perfectly chaotic world of men and freight, but were they not forewarned of our imminent arrival? I upbraided the captain, a rough-hewn brute of a man, no doubt the veteran of much trafficking. He bared his stumpy tobacco-stained teeth – presumably a greeting in his private language – and feigned surprise that we should be concerned with such trifles. Furthermore, he made little effort to disguise his disapproval of this sudden inbreak of distressed women. I pray that he be discovered the worst fellow on the whole property, for any more detestable than he I hope I shall never have to suffer.

In the coming weeks and months my observations, for good or ill, shall be set forth in a journal. It is hoped that by the time I return to these beloved shores I shall have a record of all that I have passed through, so that I might better recount for the use of my father what pains and pleasures are endured by those whose labour enables him to continue to indulge himself in the heavy-pocketed manner to which he has become accustomed. There is, I suspect, small virtue in leaving one's creatures to the delegated dominion of some overseer or manager. Perhaps my adventuring will encourage Father to accept the increasingly common, though abstract, English belief in the iniquity of slavery. It is these days heard abroad, and argued with much vigour, that the lordship over one's own person is a blessing far beyond mere food and shelter. However, to many of these *lobbyists*, slavery is simply a notional term to be equated with whatever propaganda they have read in prose or verse. It is therefore unsurprising that despite the outcry raised by their communal voices, there remain many persons scattered throughout our kingdom who inwardly cling to their old prejudices, and secretly mourn over actual or designed reforms.

And so I prepare to leave England which, with all its faults, still bears the title of 'my home'. My heart is heavy and even the prospect of new and more beautiful scenes cannot altogether relieve my sadness.

O my country, I have no pride but that I belong to thee, and can write my name in the muster-roll of mankind, an Englishman. If thou wert ten times more cloudy, and rainy and bleak, I should still prefer thy clouds and thy storms to the spicy gardens of the Orient.

The chamber to which we are confined is no more than six or seven feet wide with a narrow plank – this is the only way I can describe it – protruding from each side wall, and a thin gap in the middle which barely allows one to describe a full circle without bruising knees and legs against these *beds*. Attached to each *bed* are straps of rope. We have been informed that these are to lash us in of an evening irrespective of the weather appearing clear or inclement.

Sea terms: WINDWARD, whence the wind blows; LEEWARD, to which it blows; STARBOARD, the right of the stern; LARBOARD, the left; STARBOARD HELM, when you go to the left; but when to the right, instead of larboard helm, HELM-A-PORT; the TILLER, the handle of the rudder; the CAPSTAN, the weigher of the anchor; the BUNTLINES, the ropes which move the body of the sail, the BUNT being the body; the BOWLINES, those which spread out the sails and make them swell.

Out on deck Isabella and I surveyed the dingy sky. It promised rough sea, sudden squalls and a stormy passage. Littered about us were a company of squealing porkers and their suckling infants, who I assumed would provide us with some sustenance during the voyage to come. There is with us a small carrot-headed cabin-boy who has brought with him for companionship a pit-bull terrier, whose legendary ferociousness of spirit is likely to be tried by the larger and more exuberant porkers. One can only hope that the terrier is able to fend for itself, for already my Isabella has been obliged to dispense saline drops to the boy and accompany him back to his cot. This voyage is to be his début, and if custom is maintained it will no doubt be the first of many, until merely a few years hence he will have *sea legs*, as opposed to *land legs*, and find it difficult to reside in a world that is devoid of motion.

Isabella awoke at the dead of night and accused me of betrayal, prosecuting me with the evidence that I had managed to achieve sleep in this incommodious hole to which we have been condemned. She complained of feeling the motion sickness, of throbbing temples, burning head, freezing limbs, feverish mouth and a nauseous stomach. There was little that I could do except listen to her pitiful moaning and study the sound of the men's feet moving backwards and forwards at the helm, as the ship was now fully engaged about her business of traversing the ocean. Moments later a cock, the harbinger of day, informed me and others unfortunate enough to lie awake that it was a new dawn. Much as I desired a dish of tea, I found it impossible to prevail upon the ailing Isabella to furnish me with such a luxury. I decided to venture in search of the cabin-boy, or some other assistant, who might help me slake my thirst, and I abandoned my poor servant to her cot.

What a strange manner of men are these captains. There is little wind yet we are being blown hither and thither like a kite in the sky. Meanwhile our leader protests that the vessel's motion is so gentle and smooth that one might play bowls on deck. He claims that the waters, while not displaying the mirror-like surface upon which one hopes that all such journeys should commence, are truly becalmed. I had to question myself as to whether we were speaking of the same waters. Having procured a dish of Indian tea, I was wont to hammer my teeth on every occasion I lifted it to my mouth. The captain informed me that were there more wind we would ride these waves in easier style, but at present, at least to my observations, we were forced to rise and fall like a cork according to Neptune's whims.

Sea terms: RATLINES, the rope ladders by which the sailors climb the shrouds; the COMPANION, the cabin-head; REEFS, the divisions by which the sails are contracted; STUNSAILS, additional sails, spread for the purpose of catching all the wind possible; the FORE-MAST, MAIN-MAST, MIZEN-MAST; FORE, the head; AFT, the stern; TO BELAY A ROPE, to fasten it.

The air has turned bitter, and the rain merely dribbles and denies us the spectacle of a cascade. The sailors have found some difficulty in surviving their watch, and I am unhappy to report that three have already been consigned to the ocean, their hardiness expiring in these trying conditions. As for Isabella, I fear the worst. Her malady has assumed a more active appearance. In our kingdom we have a *quack* who claims to have some formal training in medicinal science, but he is unable to pronounce upon her condition beyond useless generalizations that a child might deliver upon a cursory glance at the poor creature. His parting advice was to *inform* me that sea-sickness soon masters us all. I am truly distressed to see Isabella in such a plight and can discover nothing to give her relief. Both food and physic have been employed to little purpose. Nothing will sit on her stomach, and through the night she thrashes about her cot as though intermittently possessed by the devil.

This morning, as though nature were bestowing a gift upon us, a fair wind rose and a gentle gust filled our sails and ushered us forward with most marvellous ease and swiftness. But she did not stop there. The gust become violent, the face of the sea grew ruffled, and waves were dashed against our stern causing the ship to pitch from side to side as though about to roll over. This wind continued to rise and punch the ocean in all directions, whilst the horizon vanished as a sheet of rain approached joining sky to sea. The distant, towering clouds were soon obscured as the heavens assumed an ominous hue of bluish-black.

I was, when this drama commenced, consulting with the captain, who took the precaution of snuffing out one of his candles and readying himself to affix the other to the table. However, before he could make it secure, the sudden lurch of the ship threw it from the table-top and for a moment we were plunged into complete darkness. And then the noise! Never did you hear such an intolerable clamour. The cracking of bulkheads! The sawing of ropes! The screeching of the wood! The trampling of the sailors! The clattering of crockery! Everything above and below all in motion at once! Chairs, writing-desks, boxes, books, fire-irons, flying all about as though emancipated from gravity's governance. The livestock screamed and grunted, causing a cacophony no less disturbing than the cries of distressed humanity. And, of course, there was always the fear that the demise of the animals might lead to hardships of diet.

I took advantage of a momentary lull and returned to my quarters, where I was alarmed at the febrile condition of my faithful Isabella. My servant and constant companion for these past twenty years, there is nobody who knows more of the sorrows and joys of my heart than dear Isabella. Since my late mother's departure abandoned a sorrowful ten-year-old girl to my father's jurisdiction, Isabella has been both mother and friend. I now cursed myself for having inflicted this voyage upon her, for her life's journey had proceeded far beyond the first fresh bloom of youth. Yet her outward vigour always seemed to belie the true nature of her advanced and advancing years. But what now? She no longer attempts to put food on her stomach, and she talks already of what we have done and passed through, as opposed to the adventures we intend to achieve at our journey's end. The captain came down to inspect his ailing passenger and left without a word, but with a grave mien painted upon his visage. It would have cost this rum-soaked man little to have advertised some outward display of affability, for his melancholy must have served only to increase the inner misery that my dear Isabella was trying so hard to conceal.

This sad night has passed with difficulty, and I am now resigned to the prospect of continuing my voyage alone. The captain asked to speak with me, and so for a few moments I abandoned my Isabella. The bluntness of this curmudgeon occasioned little surprise, but his missive took the wind from my sails. It appears that Isabella has contracted a fever common to sailors from which she will not recover. And, in order that I might be spared potential suffering, the captain insisted that come morning she should be removed to solitary quarters. Although reluctant, I could see that I had little choice but to comply with his wishes, and so I composed myself and returned to Isabella. However, the seas were once again running mountain-high, and the waves breaking with such outrageous strength that they could clearly be heard pounding against the decks. They soon punished the caulking, and by dint of some pertinacious efforts wormed their way through the exposed seams, flooding our small private world. All night we were saluted by streams of brackish water which poured over our faces.

This morning there was little relief as the clamour achieved a pitch of frightening intensity. Bright scarves of fire lit the sky, and the wind raged with unabated force. All hands were now called, not only the crew but every man or jack who could assist in this dreadful emergency. The ship was one moment being tossed up towards the clouds, the next descending with such violence that she trembled for a full half-minute, beholden to Him that her planks were still joined together. Throughout this torment, Isabella clung to my sodden hand with her weakening fingers. Then, as though involved in this thundering drama, my dear Isabella contrived to depart from this world with a theatrical flourish, so that both the tempest and her world were gone as one, and sorrow was stealthily ushered through my door. It came to pass that the sailors and myself muttered the same prayer having both witnessed a tremendous scene of suffering.

> 'At last from all these horrors, Lord,
> Thy mercy set us free,
> While in the confidence of prayer,
> Our souls laid hold on thee.'

A burial at sea is a pitiful ceremony. I cannot help but shy from describing it for fear of reviving the hurt that it occasioned to my soul. Suffice to say our lugubrious captain did his best to mutter a few solemn words, and then he had the melancholy office of dispatching the swollen corpse of my Isabella to the watery depths. Sad to recount, but she was swiftly followed by the cabin-boy, whose life never afforded him the pleasure of travelling shore to shore, and whose pit-bull terrier leapt over after him in a flight of loyalty that elicited from the scorbutic crew little more than howls of rude laughter. My schemes for the present frustrated, I therefore submitted myself to His powerful hand, and prayed that trust in His goodness would control this evil known as fate.

I took to my bed stricken with grief, but not until the carpenter had recaulked the seams so that there could be no further repetition of my aquatic night. Not only my cabin, but my life too was empty without Isabella. I tried in vain not to throw back my mind over our acquaintance, but how could I not do so? Clear two-thirds of my life had been spent in the company of this Iberian maiden who in earlier years could have given her allegiance to many eligible men. Natives of her own country, and some Englishmen, would gladly have offered their hands in marriage, and proffered their often not inconsiderable fortunes to have retained such a faithful and caring intimate. But she chose instead to remain loyal to her young mistress, whose heart beat in time to her own. Were I a poet I would compose some lines to her memory, but I am simply a lady of polite status with little talent, artistic or otherwise. I hope that one day I might persuade others to pay tribute to the greatness of Isabella. Meanwhile, my journal is now my only true companion, and the airing of thoughts and feelings that in other circumstances I might have shared with Isabella, shall henceforth form a part of its purpose.

A week ago we had the good fortune to fall in with the trade wind, and we are now careering both rapidly and smoothly upon the bosom of the ocean. The ship makes much headway, and what movement she achieves she does so steadily. The brilliant sun has chased away the clouds of darkness, and a delightful prospect confronts us. Since crossing the tropic this perfect weather has rescued me from an ague which reduced my person to lying supine and daily fearing the onset of contagion. These days it is true to say that there is not sufficient wind to fill out the sails, but there is certainly enough to render the air cool and pleasant. I have therefore passed much time on deck observing nature's new delights.

The sailors caught a dolphin, the heavenliest creature that goes upon fins, but attempted to do so without the traditional spear. A line was fastened to the stern and baited with salt-pork, but the dolphin is a large and powerful fish. Through a natural fear that this graceful beauty might break the line and flee, the decision to toss the spear was taken. This goddess of the deep was soon wrestled onto the deck where her bright colours were observed and admired, that is until the loss of blood caused them to fade and the cook made ready to prepare her for dinner. Other representatives of Neptune's family occupy us in our peregrination. The comical inhabitants of the ocean are without doubt the porpoises who gambol along both above and beneath the surface, always ready to delight with the unannounced spouting of ornamental water. Hawk-bill turtles might occasionally be espied, and they cause everybody's mouths to water. They have a tendency to idle, and it is when they are in this somnambulant state that the greatest efforts to capture them are made. But, as though with some special sense, they always contrive to awaken at just the precise moment that one is ready to haul them up and into the pot. They flick their rubbery protrusions with enviable calm, then roll and dive to the depths. Whole shoals of whale and shark are also daily visible, and as populous as sheep on the South Downs. Tropicus has indeed revealed to us a new world, the beauty of which has gone no small way to mollifying the pain which is daily lacerating my heart.

The weather has become excessively close, indeed sultry, bestowing upon us the full benefit of the concentrated rays of the tropical sun. Not a breath of wind is perceivable, and I am occasionally seized by a suffocating sensation which is only relieved when the pregnant afternoon hours finally give way to the relative coolness of dusk. I have in consequence thrown off my shop-dress and I now wear muslin, clothing myself according to the exigency of the weather. At night I lie under a solitary Holland sheet, which I have to confess is too much – yes, even this little. The crew no longer retire to their quarters at night but can be heard on deck. Before they finally submit to their slumbers, they are able to witness the phenomenon of a blood-red horizon where the sun plunges in a blaze of fire into the sea. In the morning I am agreeably saluted by the peaceful calm of a new day, but still there is no breeze to greet my clammy cheek. These early sunbeams, devoid of the noonday heat, dance playfully on the rippled surface atop which we sit. I am now inclined to bathe on deck in a large cask, but only after the crew have vacated the premises for the preservation of my modesty. I have grown accustomed to bathing myself, and executing other tedious duties, for there is nobody on board to whom I might turn and offer employment. I long to arrive in the islands, where I shall engage a servant to take up where Isabella left off.

Each day flatters with the hopes of land, but as yet nothing. I think I detect that our captain is quickly growing out of patience with the tortoise-pace that we are making, but for my part I care very little as long as we do not encounter any further squally weather. To reach my journey's end peaceably and without harm is my sole aim. Of late I have thought much of this ocean, whose breast has supported many a ship heavy with slaves. The torn roots of these *children of the sun* has occasioned the stain of *the institution* to mark first their native soil, and then bleed across the waters to deface the Americas. There will be much to discover on arriving in tropical America, but I am engaged to spend only a three-month sojourn. I am therefore set apart from those projectors who visit the West Indies to either make or mend their fortune. For one such as I, my day of departure will be dawning from the moment we espy land, and I am accordingly neither anxious nor full of trepidation.

It would appear that we have finally crawled into the Caribbean sea. This morning I was alarmed by the loud call of the morning sun and the excited cry, 'Land! Land!' Together they shook me from my slumbers. I quickly pulled about me enough clothing to render me decent, hastily fastened a dainty bonnet about my head, and dashed upstairs to join the others who stared on at the small and seemingly deserted *bird island* that we sailed close by. And then in the distance, where the horizon invited and detained the eye, I beheld our destination; a mountainous island heavily clothed in vegetation, wooded on the upper slopes, the highest peaks swaddled in clouds, an island held in the blue palm of the sea like a precious green gem. The captain confirmed that this was to be my port of disembarkation, and I thanked him for the information. He seemed surprised, clearly unused to such civility. I do believe I even detected a small bow! I craned back my head and silently praised the Lord that I had survived the passage in safety. A little malnourishment, and the development of a small feverish tendency, constituted the sum of my ailments. When set against the watery tomb to which my Isabella and others of our society had been consigned, I had indeed much cause to be grateful.

There was just sufficient wind to gently impel us forward with elemental grace towards our, or at least my, destination. The forest-garmented heights, the wheeling gulls, the careless beauty of this verdant isle, all caused my heart to quicken further her already excited beat. I retired beneath the wooden deck and prepared myself for arrival. Assembling my belongings presented little difficulty, for I had already performed much in this line in order to occupy myself during the previous few days. On returning to the deck I discovered that a negro pilot had come aboard, his negro assistant having transported him by means of a canoe evidently hollowed out of a sturdy tree of some description. It caused me a little discomfort to hear our captain immediately baptize the pilot with the title, *nigger*, but the pilot seemed somewhat resigned to his appellation.

The negro brought with him a water melon whose taste I could not suffer. It had about it a Shylocky taste of raw flesh. I preferred to watch in raptured fascination as the bluff sea-dogs devoured what was to them clearly a familiar fruit. The less ravenous, and generally more agreeable, mariners threw the lead to sound the depths. The sea adopted a lighter blue, and the negro pilot skilfully brought us around the rocks and squeezed us into the wine bottle of a bay, where the gentle plash of water sounded most musically to my ears. I was unable to perceive any exhibition of repugnance by the crew towards this black helmsman, they appearing to appreciate his navigational prowess and utmost decorum of deportment. This, to my intelligence, appeared only natural, for they were to a man generally less polished than the negro.

The beauty of the island improved as we drew nearer and found ourselves with land on either side. Hills and valleys opened on my view, and I could clearly discern that the land was dappled with trees, plants and shrubbery that were, in the main, afresh to me. However, I recognized the infamous sugar canes, whose young shoots billowed in the cooling breeze like fields of green barley, and I noted the tall cabbage palms, whose nobility of appearance provided a formidable décor to the small settlement of Baytown which spread before us in ordered and recklessly formal beauty. Behind our capital town, slender lines of houses snaked up the hillsides and merged with the vegetation. Indeed, I was beholding a tropical paradise. Our exploratory party returned with baskets full of fruit, excellent milk and fresh fowl which we consumed as our final and most succulent meal aboard the ship. This repast proved a most necessary balm to my intoxicated senses. I retired to my small cabin with a constitution for once well-watered and nourished, and a heart light with anticipatory joy at what I might witness in this new world that I had crossed the ocean to discover.

What a day! I write now on land, but my heart is giddy. I have great difficulty in maintaining my balance, veering first to the left, and then to the right, much as I did when aboard ship. It must be a curious sight to behold, but I am told that such visions are quite common, and before two days have expired my person will once more steer a true course. My last night on board the little wooden world passed most pleasantly. Having consumed what amounted to a near feast, soft slumber then contrived to seal my eyes for many an hour. If only all my nights in this cabin had passed as pleasantly it would be politic to consider making such voyages for recreation. Indeed, one might venture to suggest that such voyages could benefit the health of a traveller, instead of threatening their very existence.

In the morning I stepped out on deck as the sun cleared the horizon. We were at anchor. The view of the island that I now beheld was nothing less than magnificent. We had drifted perhaps only a further two hundred yards towards shore, but this gave one the opportunity of discerning not only general movement, but individual negro figures going about their daily business. I bade the captain farewell, and rewarded him with a small bag of coins for having delivered me safely. The truth is I wish I had a coin for every member of his crew, for my survival was more a tribute to their skills than to any act of this bellicose man, who could barely mutter a few words of thanks upon my presenting him with this token of my appreciation. I enquired as to the existence of any known family for the cabin-boy. As far as the captain was concerned there was none. And so his family lineage would appear to have reached a watery conclusion. I then raised the difficult question of wishing to know where, as near as it was possible for him to advise me, we finally committed Isabella to her grave. The captain, without even pausing for thought, answered, 'By the Azores.' He responded with such speed that for an instant I wondered if this was his common answer to all such enquiries, but I deemed it sage to hold my tongue and thank him for his information. I requested such knowledge having decided that upon my return to my native land I would erect a monument for Isabella, inscribing it with all the details of her life, and sadly her death too.

Now I was ready to leave. The negro pilot reappeared and drew a small boat up against the side of our ship. Having taken modesty into account, and having spurned all tendered help, I descended an unlikely ladder constructed of rope, and set myself in this diminutive vessel. The crew on deck applauded my feat, but I wondered if their applause signified relief at having finally abandoned this woman. They might now roister anew without consideration (if any they did show) for the presence of a lady, for these men were clearly used to treating female creatures as little more than beings of an inferior nature whose task it was merely to render service and expect in return neither gratitude nor the simplest cheering word or kindly smile. I looked back and folded my fingers in farewell, as the negro began to paddle gracefully in the direction of Baytown. He kept time and tune to his oars with what appeared to be an extemporaneous chant. As far as I was able to discern, the *song* was composed of the following words:

> *Old rum kill de captain*
> *O dear, He must die*
> *New rum kill de sailor*
> *O dear, He must die*
> *Hard work kill de neger*
> *O dear. He must die*
> *La, la, la, la, etc.*

A few yards short of the shore I discovered that there was yet another journey to be made, for it proved inadvisable to beach the small craft in such shallow waters. I therefore completed my adventure on the back of a negro. I arrived exceedingly wet and much incommoded by the surge. On shore I discovered a white gentleman whose hair was cut uncommonly close to his head. I wondered if this butchery illustrated the local fashion, but I chose to remain silent. My suitor claimed to have spent many hours waiting for my arrival, and he presented a letter of his credentials which he assured me entitled him to the honour of attending me to my father's plantation. Again I said nothing, for I now simply desired to take some rest and change out of my wet clothes. Before we left the shore the gentleman beckoned to a shoeless negro girl, whose head was buried in an old felt hat that had clearly lost its original shape. She bestowed upon me a glass of what I was informed the locals call *sangaree*, a tropical drink composed of Madeira, water, sugar and lime juice. This most refreshing drink served to increase momentarily the giddiness that I felt on achieving *terra firma*, but I was assured that its medicinal value far outweighed any unpleasant reaction that I might temporarily experience.

With the aid of my gentleman companion, I stepped aboard a carriage belonging to the estate. The carriage was light and airy and drawn by English horses. This seemed to me a needless expense, for I knew that in these parts they were blessed with perfectly serviceable horses from New England. I noted the difference between this carriage and those preferred by the negroes, whose carriages were large and heavy and drawn by mules. I further noted that the negro men wore thin-clothed apparel which left scarce anything to the imagination, and that their women wandered hither and thither barely stirring to cover their bodies. Certainly most had nothing about them more substantial than a petticoat. I imagined that in such heat as this clothing would indeed become burdensome, so I did envy the negroes their ability to dress without concern for conventional morality. However, on first encountering such a manner of display it is difficult to disguise one's revulsion.

On noticing my discomfort the gentleman at my attendance chose to enter the black throng and return with a negro woman, who was clearly a pilgrim of some sixty years. Her toothless gums were visible through her thick and open lips, and her church hat failed to mask her sad, unfeminine baldness. My factotum placed her on the backplate of our carriage and furnished her with a large fan, with which it was understood that her task would be to cool me during the forthcoming journey. And so with a black driver now in place, the gentleman seated on the rear seat next to myself, and the negro woman already gently fanning our persons, we set forth towards the estate, which I knew to be not above three or four miles to the north-west of Baytown. As we did so I bestowed a final gaze upon the good sailer which had conveyed me safely to these American shores. I am not above admitting that if one had looked closely at my visage it might have been possible to have espied a tear of sadness. This first part of my journey was over and I was breaking the last remaining link with a past that I understood. From this moment I would be entering a dark tropical unknown.

The noble English horses edged forward with an unconcerned surety of step which led me to speculate that they could have confidently negotiated an independent route to our destination. As we moved away the legion of negro people gawped and suspended whatever activity they had been engaged in. They exhibited a savage curiosity. I believe it was I who was the object of wonderment upon which their eyes were riveted, but soon we were lost from view. I struck up conversation with the gentleman, who informed me that in this place the spring does not give way to the summer, nor the summer to autumn. It is a fact that these three seasons are bound together as one, and that what we commonly know as winter makes no appearance of any kind. The heat, he pointed out, witnessing my continued distress, is something that one acclimatizes to as long as one is sensible enough to take certain elementary precautions. First of all, one must never take exercise after nine in the morning. Second, one must never expose oneself to the dew after sundown. And third, one must never take rest in a lodging house, unless of course that lodging house is managed by a trustworthy person with whom one is familiar. The gentleman insisted that his final caution was most important because of the lack of common cleanliness that one often finds among the negroes. They might be entrusted to prepare food and wash linen and so on, but only when properly trained. I made a mental note of all that he said and we progressed in silence.

The main *island road* described a route along the very margin of the sea. In some parts the waves broke in such a manner that they must regularly dampen the feet of those who choose to make their explorations upon two legs. At regular intervals we passed through a cluster of houses lacking any outward colouring, except that which they had acquired from exposure to the elements. These villages (for it would appear that this is what they were) boasted the most simple names, such as *Butler's, Halfway House, Middle Way*, etc. Although, at least to my untrained eye, these rickety structures did not appear to constitute pleasant residences, they were all positioned so that through each individual door-frame, and above every bamboo and palm-leaf fence, a beautiful sea-view was obtained.

The roughness of the road caused me a little discomfort, a sensation with which I was not altogether unfamiliar having survived my first (and I hope my last) tempest. I marvelled at the riches of the fields and thickly wooded passes to my right, and noted that the fields were divided into cane-pieces by different species of hedge, some of which to the eye alone appeared to be prickly, and in this respect I imagined would resemble our hawthorn. These West Indian fields were all neatly dressed as though preparing for turnip husbandry as practised in England. At every turn a pretty prospect attracted the eye, and these visions were made more cheerful by batches of negroes of every age and description returning from Baytown with baskets and trays and boxes atop their black mossy crowns. The critical position of these receptacles seemed not to hinder their rolling gait, nor interrupt their chatter and song. They smiled and curtseyed as we passed them by. Some chose to bestow upon us a respectful, 'How you do, misses? How you do, massa?' to which we nodded a silent reply, by which they were meant to understand that we were perfectly well, thank you.

Just after we turned off the *island road*, and into a small ascending lane, a number of pigs bolted into view, and after them a small parcel of monkeys. This took me by surprise, and I must have jumped some considerable space, for the gentleman took my arm as though to steady me and prevent my falling from the carriage. However, on resettling my position,

I discovered that what I had taken for monkeys were nothing other than negro children, naked as they were born, parading in a feral manner to which they were not only accustomed, but in which they felt comfortable. I expressed my general concern at the blackness of the native people and was corrected on one count and instructed on the other.

The blacks are not, it would appear, considered to be native people. They were, as is commonly known, imported from Africa to help ease our labour problem, and have continued to breed in these climes. Their migration to these shores means they cannot be recognized as true natives. In this same manner one cannot consider the white people native for they are here on a civilizing and economic mission. The gentleman informed me, in a short but edifying lecture, that the true natives of this region were of an Indian origin (hence the name 'West Indies'). Sadly they were discovered to be too troublesome and unused to European ways and had to be dispatched. However, this proved no simple task for, according to their savage customs, these *Carib* Indians armed themselves with clubs and sharp spears whose ends were decorated with poisonous fish bones. The character of these *Carib* Indians might best be described as fierce, superstitious and vengeful, ready to vent their anger on any and everything, animate or inanimate. Their fury bore more semblance to the wild irrationality of the lion than to the passionate intensity of man. Accustomed to being absolute masters of their own conduct, they scorned to follow orders, and displayed an implacable opposition to correction. Content merely to roam their native territory, this led naturally to the undernourishment of their powers of reasoning, and the limited development of their intellects. Presented with the improvements of civilized life they responded with apathy, continuing in that most base of all practices, the *plumping* of their fellow Indians for the purposes of consumption during their grand feasts. Happy for us that Paganism, with all its accompanying horrors, has now given way to a milder doctrine which has freed this land of the soul-sickening human feasting with which the original natives once polluted it.

Having been corrected on the count of native peoples, I was now instructed on the question of colour. It appears that there are many shades of black, some of which signify a greater social acceptability than others. My host informed me that there were other persons who could give fuller and more authoritative instruction in this matter, but generally speaking the lighter the shade of black, the nearer to salvation and acceptability was the negro. A milkier hue signified some form of white blood, and it should be clear to even the most egalitarian observer that the more white blood flowing in a person's veins, the less barbarous will be his social tendencies.

I asked after Mr Wilson, the manager of the estate and the man to whom my father had written informing him of my impending arrival, but the gentleman seemed unable to give me a clear and acceptable answer on this topic. He informed me that his status was that of book-keeper, doing so as though to plead with me that I was pressing him to stray into territory beyond his station. Knowing that my curiosity would soon be satisfied I refrained from this line of questioning and resumed the pleasant pastime of looking about myself and hoping to observe, albeit at a distance, new varieties of wild animal. But it was now that my fellow-passenger took it upon himself to broach the subject of my servant, or rather my lack of a servant. He asked of me if I was in the habit of travelling alone, careful to point out that unfettered travel can have its advantages, although he indicated that in these parts it is considered a little strange to see a lady abroad without her attendant or attendants. I suffered his polite enquiries and observations before replying as gently as possible, in order that I might spare his modesty, that my Isabella had been taken ill upon the seas and breath having fled her body she was cast upon the waters. His now flowering face and helpless stammer indicated to me the depths of his shame. I placed one hand upon his to assure him that I did not hold him in any way responsible for his blundering upon the unfortunate cause of my solitude. However, it appeared he was not to be consoled, and we passed the remaining phase of our journey without speech.

I had been led to believe that planters' residences were imposing structures which stood, if at all possible, in commanding positions to reflect the status of the person housed within. This edifice was certainly no exception. We gradually neared the end of a short and steep ascent and turned off from this treacherous path into an avenue of cedars and palmettoes. Just visible at the end of this Arcadian grove, built of wood and stone, and standing clear of the ground on broad flinty supports, was the Great House that my father could, were he to avail himself of the time, and suffer a trifle inconvenience, claim to call his own home.

The negro driver drew the carriage to a halt in a wide and somewhat ostentatious semi-circle that had the good fortune to deposit me at the foot of the sharply chiselled steps. These led up to the main entrance of this tropical palace. It somewhat disturbed my person to see no evidence of Mr Wilson. Indeed, there were no men of any description to greet me, save black servants who were all poorly clothed, horribly dirty, and had about their manner a lazy carelessness. They sauntered into view from all directions, and formed some variety of welcoming party. Both the negro men and the negro women appeared to be presided over by a *jet* woman, who stood central to this activity in a clean white dress with her arms folded across a generous bosom. She held herself as though the mistress, and stepped gaily down towards me with a delicacy which mocked her immodest proportions. She curtseyed in a charming manner, jabbered something to the driver, and then pointed to the old woman who stood upon the backplate of the carriage. I had forgotten about this woman's presence and had spoken freely and without due regard for a servant's large ears. Quickly casting my mind back over the breadth and range of my conversation, I decided that I had revealed nothing of import and felt greatly relieved by this discovery.

The large negro woman informed me that her name was Stella, and that anything I desired was to be administered by her or by persons in her charge. In common with English practices, I had expected that in the tropical family a head female servant would be employed to assist the lady in dressing, work with the needle, and attend to the bed-chamber, but clearly this Stella's duties overflowed the mould. She offered apologies for the absence of Mr Brown, although I chose not to mention to her that I had no knowledge of who this Mr Brown was or might be. She then instructed a brace of her blacks to gather my luggage, while I was made to understand that I should follow her into the house. My book-keeper bade me farewell with a short jabbing salute, which led me to wonder if he had military experience. I smiled upon him but could see that he still stung with embarrassment at having stumbled upon the reason for my unaccompanied arrival.

The entrance hall led into a central hall of handsome dimensions, both lofty and sumptuously decorated in mahogany finishing. On either side of this hall were bedrooms, and at the end of this tropical Guildhall was a wide and spacious veranda where one might sit outside and take the breeze. So overwhelmed was I by the opulence and beauty of this construction that I almost forgot my desire to rest and recover some of my senses. The firm entreaties of the negress Stella ('Misses needs must rest, must rest up some') reminded me that after the rigours of a sea journey, some moments invested in simply reclining would probably prove a great boon in better surviving the climate in the days to come, and adjusting to the social demands of the evening ahead. Stella guided me towards the bed-chamber, which was entirely fitted up and furnished in the English taste, and from whose windows I could view the sea, shipping and a great part of the island. Owing to the immodest height of the magnificent trees to the east of my chamber, I found I was also granted a most cool and merciful shade.

The bed was hidden behind the thin lawn curtains, which they describe in these parts as mosquito-nets. I am led to believe they are very necessary, for once these *gentry* smell the blood of an English arrivant they are quick to strike. Upon the bed itself lay a fine-quality Holland under-sheet, and one for covering. To the side of the bed, and neatly arranged upon a table, were quilts in case I should choose to use them. Stella advised me that often, in the middle of the night, a chill can take a sudden grip, and many an unknown visitor to those climes had been stricken (and worse) by the deception that in the tropical zone the temperature never descends. Having advanced counsel, and indicated to me these West Indian novelties, Stella informed me, with what I took to be a kindly smile writ large upon her black face, that I would not be summoned for dinner until I had rested.

It was only after this black woman's departure that I realized the true nature of my fatigue. Anticipation, the exercise and strain of such, had led me to suspend my physical exhaustion. I was forworn with travel, weary, and wanting rest. As soon as I bathed my face with water, and lay down upon the Holland sheet, I dropped into a repose so deep that it was only a stormy shaking from Stella, her hands fixed firmly about my shoulders, that raised me. 'Missy! Missy! You must hurry, hurry quick! Mr Brown, he hungry and he no wait too long for you.' And so again the name of this Mr Brown made its appearance. I determined that having travelled across half the world I would not, in my father's own house, be hurried into preparing myself to a dinner with a man who had yet to explain himself to me. How dare he demand my presence as though I were some chattel? I made myself clear to Stella, whose response was to throw her hands into the air and bellow, 'O Lordy, Lordy,' at which I instructed her to kindly lower her voice. A lady, I told her, likes to ease her way out of a slumber, and not be bullied by the mooing of a cow into this new pasture of wakefulness. I further informed her that I had no desire to hear my mother-tongue mocked by the curious thick utterance of the negro language, so she might abandon her comical jargon and adopt English. Upon this the negress apologized and said that she would wait outside. I, meantime, took pleasure in dressing and attending my toilet at my own pace. Before I describe the dinner, I will give a brief account of the environs of the Great House and elaborate on what has gone before.

The interior of the house is grand, as I said. The rooms, however, are not ceiled, and the beams protrude to afford a better circulation of air. The central hall is furnished with sofas for the purpose of relaxation, and the walls sport many prints and maps, some of which relate to navigation, a great number being of local interest and depicting the divisions of land and the breadth and extent of the estates. The most interesting of these maps is the one which shows the trafficking islands in relation to each other. I was able to discern that our own island, amply blessed with beauty, is nevertheless modest in size. Littering the central hall and the bed-chambers are any number of rockers and chests of drawers. These are all of a solid wood construction, which leads one to imagine that many fine craftsmen have clearly abandoned England to work in these tropical climes where, I can only imagine, there is a greater abundance and variety of wood, and perhaps superior quality also.

The veranda, or piazza as it is more commonly known, looks out over the estate. It is furnished with loungers and rockers, chess and backgammon boards, and a spy-glass so that one might observe in one direction the labourers at work in the fields, and in the other direction the passing of ships on the horizon. All the windows in the Great House are equipped with Venetian blinds which permit the free movement of air, and these blinds also close off some light which enables those inside to rest in cool and comfortable gloom. Beneath the house, porkers and poultry find shade and shelter and are allowed to run wild. Their retreat is well respected, but I wonder at the noise they occasion, and fear the smell in such heat. Cookery is performed in a separate building designed for this purpose but this *kitchen* is located close enough to the dining room so that during transportation the food should not be allowed to cool excessively, or be infested with insects or other pests. Some negroes appear to dwell in the hall at all times of the day so as to be near their master's call, but the majority are engaged in field-work. Their village, the sugar plant, and the attendant workshops, are all visible from the piazza. I presume that in the evening the house-servants slink away to their abodes, for there is properly no provision made for them beneath this elegant roof.

Now, in conclusion, to the dining room. Fitted out with dining table and chairs of the finest mahogany, and a sideboard charged with crystal, china plates, and silver cutlery, it is one of the most distinguished I have ever seen. The curtains are of a heavy material and fall full-length to the floor. I entered without escort and found Mr Brown, a ruddy-complexioned man whom I imagine to be in his late thirties. He was sitting at the head of the broad table, his feet upon a chair, engaged in digging out mud from the soles of his boots with, of all implements, a dining fork. Squatting obsequiously beside him, a black boy was catching this mud and hurrying to toss it out of the window so that it might not lay where it fell. Observing my entrance Mr Brown drew his person to attention, nearly crushing the poor *blackie* beneath his soiled footwear. He announced himself and came forward to shake my hand. This action marked the onset and the conclusion of this man's civility. Once more he took his seat, but his full attention was now held by the food. Stella carried out the operation of serving at table, but the normal intercourse one might expect between host and stranger was sadly lacking in this instance. For example, I remarked to Mr Brown that it was a very fine day today, to which he replied that

I would be tired of saying this before the week was over. I then observed the multitude of black servants, and commented that they all seemed good-humoured, and that I found it pleasant to observe them. His only response was to cackle rudely and attack his meat with renewed vigour, as though it might quit his plate were he not to impale it.

There is little more I can recount of our dinner with reference to conversation, for this man's ignorance knew no boundaries. I asked after Mr Wilson, which elicited mocking laughter. He announced that once I had rested he would speak with me of the affairs of the estate. I chose not to press him, having already made up my mind that immediately I could obtain ink and paper I would insist to Father that this arrogant man must go. My peace of mind was further disturbed by the sudden intrusion of a negro woman who it would appear had station above Stella. She momentarily took a seat at the table and whispered into the ear of this Mr Brown. Then she smirked and took off again without so much as a 'Good evening, ma'am' to myself, or a 'By your leave' to anybody present. Stella appeared to tolerate the insubordination of this black wench, but I had already determined upon a meal of inner contemplation dignified by an outward display of stern resolution

Of the meal itself there was little with which I could find fault, except perhaps its extravagance. The table is clearly one of wasteful plenty, in violation of all rules of domestic propriety. I have never seen such rich and heavily seasoned food: land- and sea-turtles, quails, snipes and pigeons, doves and plover. Excellent port, pepperpot, and then heavy vegetables which bore some resemblance to potatoes and cabbage, but were only near-cousin to these familiar staples of my diet. Dishes of tea, coffee, bumpers of claret, Madeira, *sangaree*, were all to be followed with citrus fruits and tarts of pine-apple. I did enquire of Mr Brown if such a banquet were usual, to which he nodded as he pushed another stewed fish into his mouth. I could only imagine that he eats but once a day. For my part I must confess I found such excesses vulgar.

The service provided by the blacks was decidedly tardy and bore little relation to the luxury of the food. Stella's charges seemed to find it convenient to set the dishes on the table in a careless and crooked fashion. Silver flagons kept company with cheap earthenware, and many of these servants and assistants (there appeared to be one for every dish upon the table) wore nothing upon their feet and salivated as they observed us eating. The busiest among them were those who drove away swarms of hungry flies with the slow, rhythmical swaying of the great palm leaves. For the rest this was an opportunity to cast greedy eyes on what they would no doubt later wolf. I regarded their teeming presence with great distaste and vowed that in the morning I would bring up this surplus with Mr Brown.

It is indeed sad that my first day should have ended so unpleasantly. Perhaps it is too much to expect an immediate adjustment to the ways of the tropics, but surely good manners rise above clime and conditions. Outside, in the darkness, I can hear unfamiliar noises. The sawing of the mosquitoes I am already accustomed to, as I am too with the grunting and squawking of poultry and pigs beneath my chamber. But the distant braying of what I imagine to be negroes, and the ghostly silence of the house about me, leads me to wonder where exactly Mr Brown's quarters are, should there be aught to trouble me. O how I miss my Isabella. Should I encounter difficulty in sleeping there is nobody to whom I might turn.

These past three to four weeks have been the most difficult I can recall. To be more accurate, the most difficult I cannot recall, for my memory of them has been clouded by fever. Although still far from being hearty, I am so much improved, I imagine that if anyone who saw me a week ago were to look upon me now they would not believe me to be the same person. As to the origins of my illness, at first I thought it some slabbery thing that had caused my stomach to stand up. After all, the table on my first night was brimming with fowl, fish and vegetables with which I was unfamiliar. But my stomach stood up and lay back down again, and still the fever had me in her grip. It was at this juncture that I succumbed to a real fear that I might have contracted the same distemper which carried off Isabella. Stella summoned the doctor, who worried that I might fall a rapid sacrifice to this climate. Accordingly, he redoubled his attentiveness to me. It was shortly after the arrival of the doctor that I lost all recollection of what was taking place about my person. Now I am improved and instructed to take great care of what I put to my mouth. I must, in addition, observe a strict diet of short walks to help rebuild my strength.

Since recovering my senses I have had the opportunity to speak with the physician, Mr McDonald, a Scotchman, who has the good fortune to practise one of the two professions, the other being the law, which offer great opportunities for those who would seek to amass a fortune in this remaining part of our American empire. An intelligent and humane man, he held my interest with his account of the qualities of tropical life, and the characteristics of both the slaves and the whites, as he had observed and experienced them. He informed me that an important branch of his duties involves caring for the blacks of various estates. There is upon every estate a hospital (or sick-house as the negroes sometimes term it) for the treatment of ailing blacks. The most common diseases of the negro are slight in comparison with those that daily threaten the unseasoned white population. Disorders of the stomach are often caused by the consumption of unripe cane which, though full of sweet juice and palatable enough, is not to be relished by those who must of necessity retain their power to stand. The negro child is easy prey for the disorders of the small-pox, measles, and whooping cough. The earlier a child takes these disorders after it is weaned, then the sooner it can grow tall and straight having passed the principal diseases attendant to its youth. Perhaps the most disturbing of all the diseases related to me by Mr McDonald was that occasioned by the discomforting attentions of a small insect known as a *chegoe*, or *jigger* as the negroes express it. This creature buries itself in their feet, and if not extracted in time nests and breeds in the flesh. Some indolent beings allow these insects to attain such a size that it is impossible for them to be taken out. They feed upon the flesh, sometimes with mortal consequences. The more fortunate are obliged to suffer amputation, often as far as the knee.

Mr McDonald is required to visit each estate once a week, for which he receives an annual stipend depending upon the number of blacks in his charge. Should he have to perform additional services, such as amputation, then he is free to make extra charges. Naturally, he serves several proprietors, so that many hundreds of blacks are under his stewardship. And, of course, he will make heavier charges for the servicing of whites, which demands closer attention. Unfortunately, the greater part of a tropical doctor's life is squandered on the bizarre imaginary diseases with which the negro claims to be suffering. Monday morning is a great time for the lazy or ill-disposed negroes to gather together at the sick-house, with heads tied up, groaning as though in terminal agony, eyes barely open, one leg dragging after the other. 'Massa, me bones do hurt me bad – me eyes turning in me head so.' Such sentiments are terminated by a long and mournful howl, as the black strives to effect his lazy deceitful purpose, which is to lie at ease in the sick-house. Most will happily irritate and keep alive old sores, inflict fresh ones, take nostrums of their own making, anything to excuse idleness. The most foolish cure to prescribe is the offer of castor oil, for most blacks so enjoy its texture and taste that they will happily fry fish and plantains in it. Mr McDonald sighed with exasperation as he recalled the woes of his profession, for it appears that far from being a sickly race, the negroes are in general muscular and robust, never fearful of the heat (although a chilly day renders them miserable and much desirous of a glass of *massa*'s rum). Erect and well-formed, their quality is attributed by Mr McDonald directly to their lack of tight clothing, which in infancy and childhood can lead to deformities among white and civilized people.

The prospect of such easy wealth has attracted many *quacks* and under-qualified physicians to these islands, but as yet there is no thorough means of checking a man's credentials should he step from a ship and claim the title of *Doctor*. Mr McDonald, however, seems ably fitted for the office, and to be acquainted not only with the frontiers of his profession, but with the personal business of this populous island, both black and white. His medical conclusion was that a book of medical treatment, especially of such diseases as are incidental to tropical climes, should be kept on every West Indian property. His recipe for white survival was as follows: to avoid exposure to the sun, eat sparingly, avoid mixing wines and fruits, take no coconut water, malt liquor or cider, eat a fair proportion of animal food or fish, and take at least two to three glasses of Madeira every day. Fear is the greatest dispatcher, but after the first rainy season the Englishman is seasoned, although some beneficial exercise beyond the sun's rays is to be recommended. According to Mr McDonald the climate of the West Indies is still spoken of with dread by those who have never crossed the Atlantic, and by others who have lost relatives through imprudence. There is in this *grave* talk much exaggeration and a good deal of ignorance. Mr McDonald's conversations were warmly welcome as I lay prostrate and panting on my bed, unable to find sleep, yet not so enervated that I was unable to pay attention to his finely chosen words. Clearly this was a man of impartial mind who would neither herd with the unprincipled whites, nor rally the blacks for their self-evident inferiority.

Stella is yet another who seems extraordinarily well qualified for the role of dutiful and patient attendant to the infirm. Of her pedigree there appears to be nothing that one might term unusual. Her mother was born a slave in these parts, but of her father she claims to know little, believing him to have been sold off to another estate. Perhaps this is her *black* way of disguising some greater embarrassment? A fine breeder, her three surviving children have long since been scattered to distant plantations. When she speaks of her lost children, Stella adopts the familiar doting tones of a mother, wishing to see them grown into strong and responsible men, but sadly having little notion of their present whereabouts or their moral or physical well-being. The father of these children remains a mystery, but I suspect strongly that the three siblings do not share the same paternal blood. According to Mr McDonald negro relations would appear to have much in common with those practised by animals of the field, for they seem to find nothing unnatural in breeding with whomsoever they should stumble upon.

An indication of the looseness of negro morals might be derived from an examination of how easily they appropriate titles which in our world have a deep and proper meaning, but in theirs appear to be little more than mere sport. For instance, among negroes it is almost an affront to address those with whom one is familiar by their name without first affixing some prefix of relationship. So it was, even before the onset of my tremulous condition, that Stella asked me if I might address her as *Aunt* Stella. Well, you might imagine my surprise at this request! I had no hesitation in refusing. After all, my aunts Mabel and Victoria bore no relation, physical or otherwise, to this ebony matriarch, so how could I bind them together with the same word? For a few moments Stella fell into a melancholy, and then, understanding that I was unlikely to change my mind, she reclaimed her humour.

It was Mr McDonald who informed me that during my illness, when comprehension of the world about me was beyond my powers, dear Stella would always be the first to volunteer to sit with me, often right through the night and to the detriment of whatever duties she might have back at her hut. Hers was the voice that first greeted me as I returned to consciousness. She whispered in hushed joy, 'Me misses, me hope you live long, very long; me hope you live to bury all your pickaninnies.' Friendship is a plant of slow growth in every climate, but it would appear that Stella and I are flying in the face of *mother nature*. These days we often engage in close conversation for anything up to an hour's duration. One of her favourite subjects is the retelling of the joys of her life, lest I should be in any confusion as to her desire to remain a slave upon this estate. 'For yam [eatables], misses, me got rice, me got salt-fish and fresh meat — and misses, now and den, me get ripe plantain and banana . . . Misses, Buckra very good, plenty for yam [to eat], plenty for wear; Buckra-man rise early, but me no like de morning; and nigger no like cold.' My veneration for this dusky maiden ever deepens, and by the day I grow increasingly respectful of her honesty with a frail visitor such as myself.

Stella's loyalty is, I am led to understand, typical of her people. It would appear that Mr Wilberforce and his like have been volleying well wide of the mark, for the greatest fear of the black is not having a master whom they know they can turn to in times of strife. The knowledge of who and where one's master is affords the black status. 'You belong no massa' is a contemptuous reproach of the highest order. I have been constantly subjected to the glozing of these dark helots on this very same subject. 'What for me want free? Me have good good massa, and when me sick, massa doctor come and physic me. Me no want to leave massa.' 'Free, misses! What for me wish to be free? Me work till me die for misses and massa. Lord have mercy, I no want to leave massa!' Such sentiments are delivered with considerable affection, and more than one imploring dark clasp has been laid upon my dress to solicit my attention to the misery that would ensue should they be spurned. The blacks are so well aware of the comforts that are to be enjoyed under *massa*'s rule, that many, particularly those beyond the prime of life, will never accept manumission. That Stella is able to wait hand and foot upon the absent *massa*'s daughter gives her additional status, although I would imagine it difficult to augment her already high rank on the estate.

I am not yet more than superficially familiar with the negro stock, but from my observations of those blacks who flit in and out of my chambers, from my talks with Mr McDonald, and from my close acquaintance with Stella, I am able to set down a few preliminary truths about the origins and subsequent behaviour of these creatures. Before the abolition the Africans arrived in these parts in a state of complete nudity. This cargo of livestock could be as large as two hundred and upwards. Merchants gathered by the dockside and purchased the negroes as they would horses or mules. Some owners had a fancy for maiming their African slaves, some branded them, pulled out some teeth, or wounded them a little with shot, while others wished them whole in order that they might *stud* the stock. The ending of the trade means that there are littered about these shores fewer and fewer Africans. Those that remain are daily wearing out and dropping to the ground, so that today the great majority of the negroes are *creoles*. In England the term *creole* is generally meant to describe those of mongrelized origins, but here the term refers to any, black or white, who is either well-seasoned, and thus deemed to have safely entered this new tropical life, or has been born in this zone and is therefore a full participant in the day-to-day commerce that surrounds the production of American sugar. One important advantage of this *creolization* of the negro is that the pure African has a far greater tendency towards madness and eventual suicide.

Clearly the negroes cannot be silent, for they talk indefatigably, and in spite of themselves, and in all seasons. Whether joyful or grieving, they find full employment for the tongue. They often choose to speak with themselves, answering their own questions and maintaining different characters, rather than fall victims to silence. The loquacious tongue of the *creole* negro boasts much bad dialect, but that of the African is

almost unintelligible and requires abundant patience if it is to
be understood. Although it originates in English and displays
many striking expressions, it is so uncouth a jargon to those
unaccustomed to it, that it is almost as if they were to speak
in one of their divers native tongues. They talk long, loud,
and rapidly, but seldom deliver anything of import. Every
passion known to man acts upon the negroes with the strangest
intensity; their anger is sudden and ferocious, their mirth noisy
and excessive, their curiosity audacious.

Unfortunately, I have heard several reports, some indeed furnished by negro servants themselves, that the black is addicted to
theft and deceit at every opportunity. The average negro would
not feel out of place in London's infamous thieves' kitchen of
Seven Dials. His thievishness is more than a match for all the
laws that can emanate from any parliament, and even when
apprehended in the act the black will invariably fly into a
passion if you refuse him the honour of being able to take
up the book and swear to the truth of what he knows to be
false. This prevalent knavery is considered by many negroes
to be no crime so long as it passes undiscovered. So adroit
are they in this that the shame lies in their being apprehended
rather than in the act itself. Sad to say, this pilfering habit is
apparently engrafted unto them by elder negroes, who consider
the teaching of ingenious theft a most necessary part of their
parental duties.

I have already commented upon their love, which is no
more than brutish gratification of animal desire. The negro
father, having been deprived of authority and power over
his children, and wielding no responsibility for their welfare,
is the least attached to his offspring. The mother, upon whom
the child is dependent for nourishment during its first year, is
by natural law party to a deeper involvement, but none of the
sacred responsibilities which ennoble the relation of child to
parent is present in this world. Unfettered by requirements of
support and education, the grace of the parental affections is

lost to both father and mother, and it becomes mere breeding, bearing, and suckling, and nought beside. Without wishing to gloss over their errors, I must acknowledge that negroes appear to be generally good-humoured in the highest degree, though untempered to the civilized ways of man.

This evening I took a recuperative walk in the company of my faithful Stella. The air had been cooled by the constant breeze, and we were not in the least incommoded. I had the opportunity to admire at close quarters the lofty cedars which surround the Great House and relieve it somewhat from the intense heat. I was also fortunate enough to be able to witness the negroes at work and play, their behaviour being interpreted with a suitable commentary by Stella. The first negroes I met were those returning from the mountains, some riding donkeys, some on foot, all laden with hampers of provisions. By law they are allowed only every other Saturday for the purpose of cultivating their mountain-grounds. By allowing them more time, especially during the slack season which we have now entered, they grow fond of their cultivation and are likely to raise more food for themselves and their offspring, thus relieving the estate a little from the heavy burden of feeding as well as clothing them. Also, if they are encouraged to visit more than the permitted once a fortnight, they bring back smaller quantities of goods and are much less likely to be cajoled into selling their surplus to passing *free* blacks, thus depleting their own stocks, weakening their constitutions, and in consequence reducing production on the estate.

The negroes in the field, including two batches of small black fry, were fast approaching the end of their day's labour and readying themselves for the short march back to the negro village. Each group of ten negroes is supervised by a driver, who walks behind, bearing both a short and a long whip. Above them all is the Head Driver, who carries with him the emblem of his rank and dignity, a polished staff upon which he can lean. He is the most important personage in the slave population of an estate, and it is he who takes daily charge of the *great gang*, which is comprised of the most powerful of the field-negroes. Ideally, he should be an athletic man of respected character, clean in his person and habits; if possible a *creole* long used to field-work, one marked out for his sobriety, patience and general civility. Most important, he should always show respect towards white people, and suffer no undue freedom of conversation or indulgence in trivial humour from those beneath him. A negro-man such as this must indeed be difficult to acquire. As they began to march I made note that male and female were naked down to the waist, and I could often observe where the application of the lash had sculpted a hideous pattern of weals upon their broad black backs. The *children of the sun* are mortals, and accordingly possess their share of failings and must endure the crack of the inhuman whip. But its use must be judicious, for there can be little more offensive to the human spirit than to observe the cattle-whip being inflicted with all the severity of vindictive malice. This, I must admit, I was unfortunate enough to witness, the villain bestowing the rope's-end being none other than Mr Brown.

This coarse man had before him a black Hercules of a brute who far outweighed and outspanned him. They stared at each other, their hatred undiluted, but the grey-haired *blackie* displayed no hint of trepidation at what might follow. In the distance his fellow field-workers trudged on towards the village, reluctant to turn their heads for fear of what they might witness. However, not for one moment did I doubt that their pounding hearts were not with their refractory fellow negro, and if I am to be honest I would have to add that theirs were not the only hearts whose sympathies leapt instinctively to this poor unfortunate. And so Mr Brown raised and cracked his cattle-whip, and in a moment down dropped the aged black upon his knees. But still he stared up in defiance, his dark eyes bright in the sun. Stella shook her head and seemed loath to answer my questions as to the cause of this brutality. All I could obtain from her was the intelligence that the black has a history of insubordination, and that *massa* foolishly seeks to make him more ruly by inflicting stripes. Again the crack as the whip struck the poor wretch, whose very posture made plain that he would sink no further unless the very sky should tumble down upon him. Once again Mr Brown raised the whip in his hand, but the negro, although well acquainted with its weight, steadfastly refused to flinch away. I asked Stella if it was common for Mr Brown to administer such flagellation. Could not one of his white assistants do this with more propriety? Stella answered that, 'Massa like to punish bad niggers himself, den dey know who Buckra be.' I could do no more than nod my head.

I was by now ready to abandon this remedial walk abroad, but Stella insisted that I should see something that might help to revive my ailing spirits. And of course she was correct, for indeed I have never witnessed so picturesque a scene as a negro village. Each house is surrounded by a small garden, and the whole village criss-crossed by miniature lanes bordered with sweet-scented flowering plants. The gardens of the negroes are not like the kitchen-gardens of England, planted with functional, plain vegetables, and the odd shrub of gooseberry or patch of strawberry. No, the negro grows his provisions in his mountain-grounds and harvests them once a fortnight, as I have described. These village gardens are decorative groves of ornament and luxury, and filled with a profusion of fruits which boast all the colours of the rainbow from the deepest purple to the brightest red. If I were to be asked if I should enter life anew as an English labourer or a West Indian slave I should have no hesitation in opting for the latter. It seems to me manifestly worth abandoning the propriety and civility of English life for the pleasant clime of this island and the joyous spirit which abounds upon it. One can always devise ways to feed the intellect, but how many of us neglect the soul, the inner self who too quickly becomes desiccated.

In this country there is scarce any twilight, and in a single moment all nature seems to falter. All nature, that is, apart from the negroes, who take this opportunity to enjoy, under the cover of darkness, their favourite pastime of dancing. It is impossible for words alone to describe what these people achieve with their limbs and faces. To me their movements appeared to be wholly dictated by the caprice of the moment, but Stella informed me that these dances obey regular figures, and that the least mistake, or a single false step, is noticed by the rest. They have dances which represent not only courtship and marriage, but being brought to bed. The musical instruments to which they leap and shake are Ebo drums, whose beat is made more harmonious by the accompaniment of a black who rattles a bladder stuffed with a parcel of pebbles, while yet another holds a piece of board upon which he beats two sticks. The principal part of the music is vocal, with one girl singing a verse and being answered by choral cries. To make out either rhyme or reason was impossible, and Stella seemed loath to offer me assistance. By this I assumed that the songs were about *massa*, and were perhaps too ironical in tone to be comfortably translated. Such a noise I never did hear. Having begun shortly after sun-down, the blacks, Stella informed me, might continue their revelry until the first peep of day. This being the case it was deemed judicious that I return to the Great House and take my rest.

I tarried a little before leaving, so that I might observe the first part of the negro feast, which is generally roasted upon three cunningly positioned firestones. The blacks choose not to adopt our plates or cups, preferring to hold their victuals in a *calabash*. This calabash is nothing more than the nut of a tree cut in half and scraped clean, but it would indeed be cruelty, not generosity, to instruct them in the use of more civilized custom, and compel them to set aside that which gives them harmless pleasure. Not for the negro the usual Christian joint of mutton – leg, shoulder or saddle. Their meaty diet is principally pork and bacon, which is a most welcome addition to their mainly farinaceous fare. But on this evening what a spread of ostentatious edibles! Breadfruit was much in evidence, it being a starch vegetable newly landed in these parts by the now infamous Mr Bligh in the hope that its presence might reduce the necessity to consume so much flour. (The English potato appears not to have taken hold here, so our *Mr Breadfruit* enjoys its ascendancy.) The chunks of sheep's flesh were identifiable by the eccentricity of shapes in which they had been dissected – diamonds, cubes, rhomboids. These were gormandized whole on their appearance, as was the parcel of *tum-tum*, boiled plantain that had been beaten in a wooden mortar and sculpted into something resembling a pudding.

The chief delights, greeted by the negroes with much bird-like screeching, were the feet and head of numerous hogs, dressed in the following manner. The component parts are cleaned until white, and then boiled in briny water until the meat falls away. Cold lime juice is applied, along with another dose of salt-water, and an abundance of country peppers. This favourite dish is intended to be consumed with cassava bread, and is known all through the region by the name of *souse*. For my own part I looked on with revulsion as these cannibals clamoured to indulge themselves with this meat, and I wished that with the growth of civilization in the negro, the gorging of such unacceptable swinish parts might soon cease.

As they bolted their food, the only interruption the negroes were prepared to suffer was that which involved the consumption of yet more drink. They grew perceptibly less inhibited as pailfuls of sugar and rum vanished down their throats. Even as I looked on it was clear that many were already overflowing with toothy pleasure. Glassy whites of eyes and grinning grinders shone in the flickering light. It was evident that within the hour there would not be one person, man, woman, or child, young or old, who would not be helplessly drunk. Indeed, even as I moved to depart an old woman stumbled and fell headlong across a bench, crashing to the ground in a manner which would have shocked the delicacy of even the most immodest

European on-looker. Stella informed me that such revelry generally terminates in a quarrel, with much brandishing of hands, clamour of the tongue, and violence in the air.

I have grown accustomed to eating alone in my chamber, not wishing to risk another encounter at the table of Mr Brown. Today I happened to glance at my calendar and realized that nearly one half of my time on this island had passed without my yet having written my *observations* to Father which will, I hope, be received as recommendations. As strength surges back into my body I will have to seize the initiative and engage with the affairs of the estate. Furthermore, I must attempt to unravel the mysteries which envelop the secretive white populace about me, the cruel Mr Brown being the chief enigma. I am continually disturbed by a reedy scraping from beneath the house, which I feel sure is more likely to be rats than poultry. Stella informed me that the best mode of extirpating rats is with terriers. Sadly, those imported from England soon grow useless, their eyesight weakened by the sun. Their *creole* puppies, although provided by nature with a protective film over their eyes which effectively secures them against this calamity grow less inclined to terrorize the vermin than their forebears.

This evening a gloom seemed silently to overspread the sky, and the white-robed clouds adopted a darker hue. Then the wind raised her pipe and a burst of heavenly dew somewhat cooled the air and chased away my feathered favourites. Out at sea the bold columns of rain began to evaporate into a grey misty shroud, while back on land this brief watery interlude occasioned the fire-flies to come forth. Outside my bed-chamber the hedges were all brilliant with their presence. In the day they are merely torpid beetles of a dull reddish colour, but at night fire proceeds from two small spots on the back of the head. The fire-fly requires motion to throw out its radiance to perfection, and when it does so it is as dazzling as any emerald. On full wing it appears the most beautiful speck of coloured fire that the naked eye might behold.

I stepped out into the night to breathe the delicious mildness of the air, and to refresh my spirit. The scene presented a fine and noble appearance, and I found many stars visible that in England would require the aid of a telescope. Queen of this heavenly vision was the moon, whose rounded image slept undisturbed on the surface of the sea, a bright saucer of pure light. The great watery weight of the ocean unfurled upon the white sands in a sweet and measured rush, and closer to *home*, and against the purple curtain of the night, active bats of every size and shape flew erratically in search of their prey. These bats are inclined to visit unannounced through the open windows of any unattended house, so I ventured inside and drew the blinds in my bed-chamber closed. Outside, the crickets and frogs raised their inharmonious voices, while inside those disgusting pests of the West Indies, the cockroaches, made themselves ready to crawl over floors and ceilings. Insect life appears to be altogether more gigantic than in England, for these troublesome ogres achieve extraordinary size, dashing themselves against lamps with great force, and occasionally slapping one most disrespectfully about the face. The monstrous chorus of the abundant mosquitoes declared these imps' intent to inflict torment. Happily this buzzing fellow's presence completes the menagerie of tropical pests with whom we unfortunates are forced to dwell.

It would seem that in these parts the arrival of a guest offers much-needed contact with the outside world, and helps break the routine of daily existence. Therefore, my presence is an event of consequence amongst the whites of this island, though of course, because of my ailment, few have had the opportunity to acquaint themselves with me. Now that it appears as though I might be regaining some little strength, Mr McDonald has taken it upon himself to visit with more frequency, which gives me much pleasure. My feeble attempts to disguise my loneliness having failed, he has chosen to bring me gifts which he imagines might help to assuage my sad solitude. The books he offers are poor enough things, for it would appear that little of quality is read in these colonies, and bookshops are quite unknown. Low and unappetizing English novels, much out of date, some of dubious moral tone, are the staple diet.

As for newspapers, we find here an even sorrier spectacle. Two newspapers issue weekly from different presses to enlighten the lettered inhabitants of what passes in this colony. They are light affairs of four to six pages, and printed on outlandishly coarse, semi-porous paper. Most columns are filled with advertisements by merchants hoping to dupe the population into parting with money for little-needed inventions from Europe. The remaining columns are filled with details of slave auctions and rewards offered for those who have escaped, or 'pulled foot', from their plantations. Foreign news is simply copied verbatim, and such items are studiously kept to a minimum. The stock *news* involves reports of the doings of local politicians, conveyed in such vitriolic and abusive language as in London would surely lead to litigation. These newspapers seemed determined to out-do the other in vulgarity of tone, freely heaping abuse without recourse to the facts. One of these sheets serves as the organ of the administration, its rival as that of the opposition. Never before have I witnessed such vicious parade of injustice and intemperance. I thanked Mr McDonald generously, without displaying my scarcely governed dislike of these *sheets*, and informed him that he need not bring these newspapers again to distress my sensibility. To be honest I would rather sink in isolation than be offered the comfort of such vileness. Mr McDonald understood, and suggested that he might introduce a colleague to lunch with us, hoping as he did to extend my social circle by degrees. I readily agreed and informed my bouncing black Stella of the impending luncheon appointment, to which purpose she immediately began to busy herself. Before I describe the dramatic events of our social interplay, it will serve to record the details of the extraordinary board that was set before us.

On account of my arising late (in consequence of Mr McDonald's instructions that I seek further rest at either extremity of the day), the board was neither breakfast, nor lunch, but no less remarkable because of this. We began with a most agreeable forenoon drink called a *beveridge*, which is made from the milk of the coconut, fresh lime juice and syrup from the boiler which, though sweet, has still the flavour of the cane. The men mixed this with a small quantity of rum, but I was led to believe that this practice was something from which ladies should refrain. This *beveridge* was presented to us in a crystal cup lidded with silver. Along with this *beveridge* we had thrust upon us baskets of fruit from which, according to our physician's maxim, one should eat as much as possible since 'fruit never hurts'. Next we had trolleyed before us ham, eggs, and various breads, the favourite of which was the cassava bread. The cassava is best described as a fleshy root, the sweet variety of which is used for food. One must take care not to consume the cassava water, or juice, for it is poisonous, but the body, having been dried and baked on thick iron plates, is both wholesome and palatable. We swilled down this noonday extravagance with tea, for coffee and chocolate are deemed too heavy to be taken under the vertical rays of the mid-day sun. We then consumed a little punch, which consisted of Madeira, port and claret. Mr McDonald also took the opportunity to sup a little Bristol beer, while his guest partook of all in moderation. Perhaps I should take this opportunity of introducing our third member, for he was to play a major role in our drama.

Mr Rogers arrived in a light carriage, together with Mr McDonald. I happened to be engaged in my bed-chamber, so Stella ushered them onto the piazza for drinks. My first impression upon joining them there and casting eyes on this new guest was to note how florid and healthy was our physician, a fact I had not considered until confronted with someone against whom I might set him. Mr Rogers is a slight man who looks as though his fifteen-year sojourn in this climate has made inroads into the health of his constitution. On my presenting myself he stood, bowed graciously as one might expect of a churchman, and after some sharp colloquy we three decided to repair immediately to our table. As we did so I noted that Mr Rogers has a tendency to cough, and he peppers his words with this dry ailment. In his case he could wish for no more suitable companion than a physician.

Mr McDonald is the dominant of the two men. Almost before we had found our seats, and begun to sup the *beveridge*, he asked after the whereabouts of Mr Brown. I said that I assumed Mr Brown to be out in the fields. I quickly seized this opportunity to pursue the question of Mr Wilson, directing my enquiries towards our new guest. My past gambits on this subject had been effectively countered by Mr McDonald with evasiveness and some outward signs of discomfort. For his part Mr Rogers simply shook his head and confessed that some not inconsiderable time had passed since Mr Wilson had taken up residence on a neighbouring island. Unless my eyes deceived me I felt sure that I detected a knowing glance, perhaps even a reproving one, pass from Mr McDonald to the other. Possibly to avoid Mr Rogers stumbling into waters from which he would prefer his friend to steer clear, Mr McDonald took the initiative and commenced a solo rendition of his feelings about the deficiencies of absentee planters, and those they leave in charge of their fortunes.

Mr McDonald contrasted the use of the phrase 'at home', when applied by the English expatriate, with its use by the French. For the former, he always means England, but the Frenchman will determine that his island is his 'home', which naturally results in his making a greater effort to ensure its moral and social survival. The English planters look upon these islands as colonies to which they are exiled for a certain period, places containing their properties, and therefore of the greatest consequence to them, but very few expect to die on these tropical estates. Those who have troubled to bestir themselves all look forward to spending their last years in the land of their birth. They never see, or inhale the fragrance of, a *creole* rose without letting their imaginations stray through the rich gardens of fair England. Mr Rogers asked if this was so bad. After all, was it not only natural that one should wish to return to one's provenance? Mr McDonald stormed this defensive position and expanded his argument thus. When, according to our physician, the decline in revenues from tropical American holdings set in, the overseas owners as a class increasingly neglected to visit the tropical zone, and some among them even to care for their personal possessions. These men of the privileged pigmentation, who eschew the slightest labour as not only painful but degrading, have of late begun to exhaust their scant credit in England, transferring their holdings to the jurisdiction of agents, managers, overseers and book-keepers. They are now happy to see their properties maintained in any way, so long as they continue to reap a small reward while some profit remains.

According to Mr McDonald the day of profitable exploitation of West Indian sugar is in its eventide, due in part to trading restrictions, and in part to the new age of industry dawning in England. Thus, fewer men of calibre are wont to appear in the tropics, and the dire consequences of abandoning control to others are everyday visible. Throughout the region places once of honour and trust are being gradually filled by medi-ocrities and scoundrels. Multiple office-holding has apparently become commonplace and is being carried out to extravagant lengths, as self-created lawyers, self-educated physicians, and venal merchants carry the day. The good doctor swears that at any moment the legislative and administrative organization of our own island is likely to collapse, and he is sure that there can be few local estates not now hopelessly entangled in debt, and indeed he insists that many are probably mortgaged beyond their real value.

It was at this crossroad that I felt I ought to remind my companions, in as pleasant a fashion as possible, of my position as the daughter of an absentee owner. While it would be true to claim that my father has a healthy annual income returned to the mother-country, and has also been known to indulge in the common practice of borrowing heavily with his trans-Atlantic properties as security, surely the fact that I had arrived to inspect the estate made him less culpable than these absentee blackguards. They agreed, but suggested that their basic argument was sound. Absenteeism was the primary cause of social breakdown, for just as one could not run a school without a headmaster, or a monarchical system without a monarch, one could not hope to run these tropical possessions without commitment to responsibility at the highest level. It was further suggested that in the West Indies the white expatriate of upper rank is liable to become simply indolent and inert, regardless of all but eating, drinking and self-indulgence. 'What is a man, If his chief good and market of his time, Be but to sleep and feed?' Mr McDonald declared. The passion with which he declaimed these lines from *Hamlet* surprised me not a little. I had not thought him so excitable. In the lower orders, they are the same, with the addition of conceit and tyranny, considering the negroes to be creatures formed merely to administer to their ease, and to be subject to their vagary. These degraded white people appear to be the offscum, the offscouring, indeed the very dregs of English life. It is near impossible, contended our physician–politician, to persuade these white people, high or low, that blacks are human beings, or that they might possess souls.

On completion of this interlude, Mr Rogers replaced upon the table a piece of bread that was already half-way lifted to his mouth, and sought clarification from Mr McDonald that he had understood him correctly. He claimed that our physician, this same man who appeared to be defending the blacks, was one who had frequently spoken otherwise of our darker brethren.

Mr McDonald smiled, and then prepared to defend himself, first by restating briefly his opinions upon the white populace in case there should have been any misunderstanding of his position. 'In short, our islands have become the midden for the detritus of the parent country.' At this point Mr McDonald paused for effect, and then continued. 'But this is not totally the fault of the white arrivant. Constant association with an inferior race will weaken the moral fibre of a white man and debase the quality of his life. A mere glance should be sufficient to convince an observer that the West Indian negro has all the characteristics of his race. That he steals, lies, is witless, incompetent, irresponsible, habitually lazy, and wantonly loose in his sexual behaviour, is apparent to even the most generous of those who would take *sambo*'s part. It is only the dread of corporal punishment which keeps these incorrigible thieves in order. To each other they display unimaginable cruelty, and when they fight they are particularly adept at kicking and biting. All attempts at mental instruction having failed, it is to be regretted that only a hearty laying on of that hateful implement, the whip, will rid them of their rebellious thoughts.'

I listened intently, and observed Mr Rogers nodding in agreement with some of what the doctor prescribed. Mr McDonald went on and claimed that the clearest evidence of West Indian moral turpitude was to be found in the social evil of miscegenation, a practice contrary to the Anglo-Saxon nature, and one that gave rise to a sub-species of hybrid. Some white men, though considering negroes little more than beasts of burden, had no objection to making these negroes partners of their illicit intercourse, and then condemning the issue of such unions to shame and degradation. The female offspring invariably take the name of *housekeeper* and in turn become the mistresses of white men, while the male offspring merely drag out an existence as scarcely tolerated spaniels permitted to lick the feet of their masters, but just as likely to be kicked out of doors on a whim. The mothers of such children face an even worse destiny, having been used by degenerate Englishmen who no doubt simply came to make a quick fortune and return rejoicing at their success. Such women are abandoned with little to sustain them socially but the significance given their litter's skin, and seldom even the most meagre of allowances. These dingy women may soon grow fat upon the bread of prostitution, and when their bodies become diseased, and their constitutions weakened by dissipation and excess, their sources of support fail, and the curse of poverty falls hard and heavy upon the afflictions of decrepit age. Their lot, truly, is wretched, more so when one considers that in the tropics, unlike England, immorality is impossible to conceal, for all is known and speedily rumoured abroad.

I must concede that there followed a few moments of silence. Both men appeared to wonder if their talk had not gone too far and had, perhaps, angered me. For my own part I felt privileged to have witnessed such a debate between two responsible men, one clearly dominant over the other and likely to win any argument by force of personality, the other gifted with a more temperate spirit, but unable to stem the tide raging against him. Mr McDonald added a *coda* to his argument, in a most witty and informative manner. The reparation of castes in India, he claimed, is not more formally observed than the careful division of shades in the tropics caused by indulgence in this miscegenation, or race-mixing. The offspring of a white man and a black woman is a *mulatto*; the mulatto and the black produce a *sambo*; from the mulatto and white comes the *quadroon*; from the quadroon and the white the *mustee*; the child of a mustee by a white man is called a *musteefino*; while the children of a musteefino are free by law, and rank as white persons to all intents and purposes.

Mr McDonald's careful definitions caused some much-needed laughter all around. The divers black attendants, who had been audience to all that we had said, brought forth the Bristol beer and punch, along with dishes of tea. To a person they displayed the virtuous animal fidelity of the dog. Mr Rogers seemed anxious to leave our contentious zone of discussion. He therefore turned the conversation upon Mr McDonald's work, and skilfully diverted it from any scrutiny of his own duties within the Church.

He inquired of Mr McDonald if he had explained to me the nature of a physician's responsibilities, and Mr McDonald asserted that he had done so. The doctor then informed us that he would gladly enlarge upon such of these responsibilities as might cause us further amusement. He re-asserted that the hospital was crowded with patients who have little the matter with them, who can only diagnose their illness as a 'lilly pain here, massa', or 'a bad pain me somewhere, massa', and who evidently visit the sick-house only in order that they might idly sit and jabber away time with friends. Of the authentic negro diseases, chief among them would appear to be lameness. It is principally as a result of the *chegoe*, that ubiquitous diminutive fly which works itself into the feet to lay its eggs, and, if not carefully and swiftly extracted, will corrupt the flesh around it. It seems the negroes are all provided with small knives for the purpose of extracting the *chegoe*, but as no pain is felt until the sore is produced, the extreme laziness of the negro frequently leads them to neglect this simple precaution. As a result dirt will enter the wound and make it difficult to obtain a cure. (Sometimes the black will go lame for life.)

The good doctor's general point about negro illness related to their cowardice. Mr McDonald asserted that in the matter of bodily pain it was not possible to be more craven than the sooty brethren. At the mere application of a poultice to a finger, or some such trifle, strong young bucks often cry out with tears running down their faces as though suffering amputation. At the conclusion of this *ordeal* the progeny of Afric's despised inhabitants are wont to clap their horny hands together, and, of a sudden, white grinders will shine bright from their black visages. This dread of medical treatment often leads them to conceal real disease, and such cowardice carries off many negroes each season. With this final observation of negro life our good doctor, having satisfied his thirst and filled his belly, hauled himself to his feet. He bade us farewell, and declared that once he had attended to his duties on a nearby estate he would send back the carriage for his friend.

Mr Rogers and I retired to the piazza, where we were able to view the good doctor riding off to repair the negroes of another owner. I felt sure that if I listened closely I might hear Mr Rogers whispering a prayer for their salvation. I looked across at Mr Rogers, having already conceived a design by which I might extract further information from our man of the cloth as to the fate of Mr Wilson and how he came to be replaced by the uncivil Mr Brown. The first strategy of this programme involved enquiring after and then listening to his deliberations upon his fellow members of the Church. His answers proved to confirm what I had suspected, that those in tropical holy orders are often lacking in both learning and piety, and serve as models of ill-conduct. Some are quite *addicted* to lewdness, drinking and gambling. Indeed, Mr Rogers suggested that some were better qualified to be retailers of salt-fish, or boatswains, rather than ministers of the Gospel. As to the reasons for this, they are two-fold. Firstly, tithes are customarily paid with produce of a decidedly inferior sort. Accordingly, emoluments vary considerably from year to year, but are never sufficient to support the superior churchman. As to the second reason, it would appear that the planters have little or no religion. The making and maintenance of money is their God, and the expenditure of time and thought upon religious subjects is deemed 'bad business'. Naturally enough, the ambitious or able minister is unlikely to be attracted to this tropical region.

With regard to the spiritual welfare of the negro, Mr Rogers felt that as a member of the Anglican Church this was not his duty. The Moravians and Methodists seemed to find some purpose to such labour, but Mr Rogers claimed that to pitch a sermon or an interpretation of the Gospel at a level base enough for the negro to understand would require a pastor with a thorough knowledge of negro customs, and modes of speech. Such a mentor would also have to instill in his charges the understanding that the emotions and intellect of the untutored savage are not those of the European, who learns from the Christian message a blessed form of self-control from an early age. A negro will one day shed tears at the plight and sufferings of our sweet saviour, and the very next day plead total ignorance of our redeemer's existence. Were one's aim to be a revolution in the moral conduct of the negro, then Mr Rogers was adamant that the *teachings* of *massa* would be of greater benefit than the *preachings* of any minister.

It was at about this time that we fell into a deep and lengthy silence. I was trying to frame my next assault upon Mr Rogers when I heard a light snore emanate from his person. It seems as though the custom of taking a rest after lunch extends to those who watch over our spiritual and moral welfare. I longed for Mr Rogers to re-awaken so that I might question him of Mr Wilson, and to this end I even toyed with the idea of asking one of the male house negroes to arouse him. However, I finally decided it prudent to let him slumber in the shade of the piazza, for the stiff sea-breeze had died away and a slothful calm prevailed. The extensive view from the piazza features an expanse of harvestable vegetation, but the higher slopes are rich with thick dark forest, parts of which I imagine could never have been trodden by the feet of man. The arrangement of the majestic trees, some solitary, others elegantly grouped, presents a picturesque scene. These trees of noble growth cover all the banks and ridges, while the master-tree, the tall coconut, moves her fronds in stately regal fashion. These giant ostrich-feather branches hung almost motionless in what little breeze remained. Down towards the coast, which from the height of the Great House appears rough and barren, are clustered numerous fruit trees upon whom I am learning to bestow a name; the sea-side grape, sugar-apple, breadfruit, soursop, pawpaw, custard apple, mango, lime, acacia, orange, guava, etc. Examples of all these trees are to be found, although I cannot as yet claim the expertise of a trained eye.

Presently the carriage could be seen returning up the steep ascent of the hill. As though aware of my intentions all along, the frail Mr Rogers only now managed to stir himself from sleep. He shook slightly, as a puppy might, and then coughed heavily so that his body trembled like a leaf. He rose sheepishly, but stood formally to attention, embarrassed it seemed at having ascended into the higher world and left me unattended in this. Furthermore, he seemed distressed that he should have re-entered this world in such an ill-organized fashion. Our contrite churchman stuttered a few words of apology, then quickly gathered his walking cane and bade me a hearty and warm, if somewhat hurried, farewell. As I watched him climb aboard his carriage I found it difficult to arrest the laughter welling up inside me. Poor Mr Rogers. After enduring the predicament of trying to contain the excesses of his friend's well-lubricated tongue, he then fails wholly to engage with his host and imposes upon her an hour or so of his slumbering silence. I wondered if I would ever again set eyes upon this man's timid face. Goodbye, Mr Rogers!

Feeling near-drained by what had already proved an exhausting and eventful day, I retired to my room to rest and prepare for my customary solitary dinner. Mr Brown had taken to dining alone, either after I had concluded my repast, or before I had begun it, according to his whim. However, I was delivered from a light siesta by a knock upon the door, which then opened. Before me stood Mr Brown, bold and unapologetic in his manner, asking if I might wish to dine with him this evening. I do not know if it was curiosity, or simply surprise that stirred me to agree, whereupon he nodded briskly and withdrew as quickly as he had appeared. The next on the scene was a joyful Stella, who bustled about as though I had in some way achieved a minor success. I resented greatly Stella's gay disposition and now solemnly wished that I had found some way to refuse Mr Brown's crudely presented offer of his company, but clearly it was too late.

And so once again I found myself at my father's table in the company of the enigmatic Mr Brown. However, I was unable to credit my senses when we were at once joined by the same insolent negro woman who, as I had already noted, seemed to exercise some authority in the house beyond that of Stella. I asked Mr Brown outright who was this woman, and had she a position which entitled her to sit with us at table. He gave no more answer than a dismissal of the intrusive black wench with a wave of his hand, as though she were some trifle. She slid out noiselessly, but not before rewarding me with a spontaneous glimpse of her white grinders. Again I demanded some explanation of this slattern's presence, but Mr Brown sighed and answered that she was no more to him than Stella was to me. I thrust iron into my voice and declared that I would never enjoin Stella to sit with me at my dining table. Mr Brown appeared unconcerned, and remarked that when I had spent more time among them I might come to understand that everything is not as in England. This dismissive response made my blood boil, though I soon recaptured my equilibrium. Having achieved this little momentum I pressed on and asked after the nature of the earlier dispute witnessed between himself and the impressive black Hercules. Mr Brown's features assumed a most weary aspect, and he set down his implements as though preparing himself for some lengthy courses of action. Either he would explode in fury, or he would patiently explain to me what I sought to know. I held my breath, for I confess I was a little nervous, unsure as I was which way he might spring, for my understanding of this man was slight. As it happened, I was to be rewarded with an explanation.

He began with a short summary of the *deficiency* laws, which

were introduced with the intention of increasing the white
element in these islands. Thus an estate could be fined for
having less than one white person to every thirty-five negroes.
The fear was of insurrection, and discipline became the chief
and governing principle on every estate. Unfortunately, these
deficiency laws proved difficult to regulate, for Caribbean emi-
gration was equally difficult to promote. Those who came were
usually the poorest sort of tradesmen and clerks, unqualified in
any type of plantation work. *Carpenters* who knew not a saw
from a chisel, *bricklayers* who knew not wood from stone,
book-keepers who were illiterate and innumerate, so that the
numbers of negroes in proportion to whites was not only
growing, but the quality of the whites was rapidly falling. Mr
Brown continued at his unhurried pace. 'The old fool you call
Hercules is the chief trouble-maker of the estate. He steals, lies
and provokes the others to acts of minor rebellion which must
be quashed at once.' Mr Brown apologized, yes, he apologized,
for any discomfort caused by my witnessing of his behaviour,
but he insisted that punishment, varying in severity according
to the master's disposition, often called for the use of the whip.
With this he rose from the table, bowed and left me to complete
my dinner alone.

I must conclude my summary of this remarkable day by
acknowledging that I am learning a little about the passions
of the white society in these parts. I will now write to Father
and tell him of my adventure. I will also relate to him the little
I know of his manager Mr Wilson (and his subsequent flight to
a neighbouring island), and inform him of the strange presence
of this Mr Brown at the helm of his estate. (Good manners will
prevent my mentioning, at this time, Mr Brown's friendship
with the negro woman.) I also feel compelled, having listened to
the words of Mr McDonald with some interest, to recommend
that Father either take a more active interest in his estate, which
would involve nothing less than a protracted visit, or find
some way of relinquishing control, for surely this system of

long-distance ownership is contributing to social anarchy in these parts.

I have received an awkward and somewhat surprising communication from Mr McDonald pertaining to last week's lunch with Mr Rogers and myself. It appears that Mr Rogers felt that his colleague's behaviour merited an apology of some form, so he persuaded Mr McDonald to set down his excuses on paper. Heat and drink, an excess of both, are his principal self-exonerations, these plus the novelty of a lady's company and the neglect of proper deportment in such circumstances. I answered briefly, dispatching the letter by way of Stella's network, assuring Mr McDonald that there was no necessity for such over-abundant apologies. If he felt that he had drunk a little too much and over-anointed his tongue, he might rest assured that he had let nothing slip which might be interpreted as in bad taste, nor had he been in any way offensive to myself. No sooner had the letter vanished from my sight than who should present himself at the door to my chamber but the correspondent himself, laden with freshly picked flowers and making supplication in a not wholly appealing fashion. I ushered my visitor back into the central hall where I promised I would soon engage with him. Stella was unable to erase the smile from her face. She took the flowers and undertook to find them a vase in which they might flourish.

I joined the good doctor and found that *imp of Satan,* Aberdeen, perched at his feet and buffing up his boots, while the young scoundrel, Westmoreland, was one moment dusting down his *massa*'s jacket and the next flicking an orange bough to keep flies and other insects from his person. I dismissed them hurriedly, and proceeded to take up my station in a lounger opposite to Mr McDonald's. I felt an unfamiliar discomposure in the good doctor's company, and thought it best myself to broach the choice of subjects. I declared myself glad that he had come to visit, but added that my time here seemed to be slipping by and still I knew little of anything beyond this estate. At this Mr McDonald seemed to find his cue. He suggested that I had almost regained full strength, and that we might explore the island in each other's company. I assured him that such a scheme might be most edifying. The project having been descanted upon and defined, we fell into silence. Then Mr McDonald rose from his chair, drew himself up to his full height and blurted out what he had truly come to deliver. As he did so his eyes glistened and his lips quivered with emotion. He warned me that Mr Rogers's affections for myself were of a not altogether honourable nature, and that I should be wary of how I might proceed with him. I tried hard not to laugh, for it was becoming apparent that both this clown, and his oafish friend, were engaged in some manner of feud for my favours, Mr McDonald being the more determined of the pair. I believed Mr Rogers's *affection* to be no more than mere fancy, whereas Mr McDonald's was evidently embossed with an altogether different stamp. I too rose from my lounger, and thanked Mr McDonald for his information. I accompanied him to the door, although his pace was somewhat too rapid for me. Having delivered his fabrication the tropical doctor wished now to escape as quickly as possible before being quizzed and discovered as a mischief-maker. I watched him until he disappeared over the side of the hill and was swallowed up by the shrubbery that clothed the rugged descent down to the *island road*.

As for Mr Brown's opinion of Mr McDonald, he had nothing to say in favour of Scotchmen. That indeed, as he made clear, was all there was to say on the matter. I asked him if it might not be possible for there to be worthy and honourable Scotchmen, but this seemed tantamount to asking Mr Brown to contemplate the existence of generous Jews or intellectually adroit negroes. Of late, as I sit on the piazza, or walk in the grounds, or recline in the central hall, or even as I take dinner, Mr Brown has fallen into the habit of appearing before me to engage in a few pleasantries. It seems as though his initial resentment at my presence has been eroded. Perhaps he has come to realize that I pose no immediate threat to the *status quo*. Perhaps the discovery that I am not the carrier of bad news has lightened his heart. He has informed me further on the fate of my father's agent, Mr Wilson. Apparently this man had been stealing from the estate and has fled to another island. Whether he so chose, or was compelled by force, is unclear. However, he no longer resides on these shores. It would appear that quite apart from petty thieving, the chief complaint against Mr Wilson was that he was not sufficiently aware of the imminent threat of a slave revolt.

This intelligence I gleaned from Mr Brown when again I made reference to his unnecessary savagery towards the negro Hercules, Cambridge. And again Mr Brown reminded me that the whites in these parts live in constant apprehension of revolt, for often the only reason negro attempts at insurrection meet with no success is their lack of any regular plan. Such eruptions occur with frequency and are met with equally fierce suppression, the latitude of punishment being curtailed only by the desirability of avoiding permanent injury to valuable stock. This negro rebelliousness has led to the need for organized militia under the command of the Governor. All whites between sixteen and sixty are obliged to serve, clergymen excepted, and troops are assembled for drilling once a month, and for manoeuvres on several days of each year. On negro play-days martial law is imposed and all militia men are required to be on duty. According to Mr Brown one of the chief sources of conflict between himself and Mr Wilson was the latter's attitude towards the organization of such militia. Apparently Mr Wilson viewed them as something of a prank, whereas Mr Brown, a man closer to the moods and vagaries of the blacks, viewed their continued existence as a matter of vital importance.

I have decided to write again to Father expanding upon the nature of this conflict between Brown and Wilson, and requesting him to investigate if in the last year there has been any marked fall in the level of profits from the estate. I would be surprised should there have been any decrease, since my intelligence tells me that for all his surliness Mr Brown knows well how to manage the negroes, and does so from what one might term *ground level* rather than by dispensing his justice or otherwise from on high. I find it difficult to comment upon white life style in anything other than general terms, for all I know comes from conversational skirmishes with Messrs Brown, McDonald and Rogers. I have, however, in the past week seen a little of negro life, and had the opportunity to converse with both black and white on this subject. The result is that I have made some observations which, ink, paper, and time permitting, I will certainly share with Father.

The negro forms the basis of the system and is of two sorts, the imported slave and the slave of local origin. It is desirable that a predominance of the former should rapidly be altered to a majority of *creole* slaves. Slaves of various tribal stock, some superior in nature, some inferior, are represented, and some tribes are better suited than others to certain modes of work. Yet with the passage of time, and inter-breeding among the tribes, the single, indistinguishable creole black emerges, who, having been in contact with whites from his birth, and having the great advantage of familiarity with only the English language, is less intractable, more intelligent, and less likely to provoke discord. He has not about him the offensive pride and natural ferocity of the African, who, having been torn from his native country, and made to toil under a burning sun in mortal fear of the lash, is hardly likely to form a favourable opinion of his masters. Memory often transports him back to his native land, where he roams in pursuit of the lion or leopard, or seeks noonday rest neath the shade of Afric's huge trees with family and friends about him, their voices raised in gentle song. Yet memories of such scenes are soon disrupted by the crack of the driver's whip, or the coarse bellow of an overseer, and the African is reduced to despair, and it is at such moments that the dark spirit of revenge enters his unChristian soul. It is to be hoped that this process of *creolization* will soon replace all memories of Africa, and uproot such savage growths from West Indian soil.

Of the servile negro class, only half of those on the plantation earn their daily bread by engaging in the culture of the cane. The rest are craftsmen, herders, nurses, domestics, or simply the infirm and aged, or the very young. Of the field-labourers a division into three groups is usually made. In the first group the big able-bodied men and the lusty women cut and grind the cane, and clear and hoe the land ready for replanting. The second gang is composed of boys and girls, those recently sick, and pregnant females, who weed and perform light tasks. The black boys are nearly all competent whistlers, their song-repertoires composed of variations on our traditional airs. Such harmonies aid their labour. In the third group are the mischievous pickaninnies, the little pack of black wolf-cubs who have free range simply to hoe and weed the gardens under the authority of a trustworthy old woman. The first two groups come under the jurisdiction of black drivers who differ from their sable brethren. For most negroes employment is abhorred and idleness sheer delight, but these *trustees* are specifically chosen for their diligence and application to toil.

The field-hand's day begins just before sunrise with the clamour occasioned by the blowing of a conch-shell. The first gang is led out to the fields by the black drivers and a white overseer, a procession of dark dreamers taking with them all they need for breakfast and work. Their most treasured and important movables are the hoe, the machete, and the agricultural fork. The list of names is thereafter called, and the names of all absentees noted, whereafter they work until nine when a break of a half-hour is permitted for the consumption of boiled yams, plantains and other vegetables seasoned with salt and cayenne pepper. By this time most of the absentees have made an appearance and are rewarded with a few stripes of the Head Driver's whip. After breakfast they continue with their labours until a bell calls them at noon, when they are permitted two hours of rest and refreshment. For the negroes this generally consists of squatting on sooty limbs while stuffing the belly, then slumbering swollen like a pig. At two o'clock they are once more summoned and at this time usually manifest signs of greater vigour and animated application until sunset, when they are released to their rum and revelry.

For hours the men will indulge themselves in gambling, *pitch and toss* being a favourite, a game occasioning loud and excitable responses, which very much suits the negro temperament. On these fine tropical nights it is possible to watch from the piazza as the negro women cook the supper and tell stories to one another. The chief meal consists of what the negroes grow and cultivate for themselves, supplemented by the two pounds of excellent salt-fish which is weekly served out to adults, with children receiving an allowance of a pound and one half from the day of their birth, and drivers a princely three pounds. Not for the hungry negro a simple cold mess to conclude a day's labour. The scent of fresh bread often flows from their ovens, and I am told that the tea they boil using the soiled waters of the nearby turbid stream is surprisingly palatable. By far the greater number of negro children happily display themselves in a state of nature. Their common form of recreation is to dance all about, after which, along with their elders, they will retire for the night unconscious of any harm until dawn, when again they are driven afield to labour. Once they reach the cane-pieces there is one strange custom which the negro seems determined to indulge in. This involves tearing off their shirts and secreting them under a bush when threatened with even the lightest rain. In this state they are wont to continue their labours, for the rain runs quickly from their oily skins. Should a negro allow dampness to enter his clothing he will almost certainly contract the tremors and fall swiftly into a decline.

Work is carried on daily except for Sunday and every other Saturday, when the slaves are free to raise their own provisions such as plantains, yams, eddoes and other tropical vegetables. They also keep hogs, rabbits and such livestock. On their free days, and the holidays of Easter, Whitsuntide and Christmas, they visit the market to sell and trade what they have cultivated. They have a keen eye for fancy articles of little practical value, and they love their free time in which to gossip on trivial matters, investing them with an almost absurd gravitas. On Sundays and holiday occasions the negro will cap his festivities by indulging a passion for dress, a love of which is curiously strong in these people. Male or female, they show the same predilection for exhibiting the finery of their wardrobes, and will generally adorn themselves in the following manner. The dandified males sport wide-brimmed hats and silk umbrellas, and promenade in windsor-grey trousers (which are generally embroidered about the seams with black cord). They complete the spectacle with white jackets, and shirts with stiff high collars. The *sable-belles* are no less extravagantly modish in their ornamental silk dresses, gauze flounces and highly coloured petticoats which, though of the best quality, display patterns more commonly employed in England for window-curtains. Those who sport bonnets blend the fiercest shades in a close companionship with each other, so that these rainbow-hats dazzle one's eyes at a mile's distance. Others seem to imagine their Sabbath toilet complete only when combs are stuck into their woolly heads, although the poor implement would be doomed should it attempt to conquer their coarse ungovernable hair. I for one take greater comfort in viewing the negroes, male and female, in their filthy native garb, for in these circumstances they do not violate laws of taste which civilized peoples have spent many a century to establish.

During the crop season those who are chosen to work in the boiling-house often drudge long into the night, and some clean through until dawn without even a momentary suspension of labour. But this is the only real variance from a pattern which the average English labourer might consider luxurious, especially if he were to view the quarters of the plantation blacks, their cottages surrounded by trees and shrubs, the interiors often plastered and white-washed, the roofs thatched with palm leaves, and the floors of the best rooms board. Their bedding is for the most part a sack filled with dry plantain leaves, which I am led to believe can prove exceedingly comfortable. Some negroes find it advantageous to drape their narrow nests with the mosquito-net so as to hinder these creatures, whose kiss is more powerful than of any English gnat or harvest-bug. Although the family is deemed the basic social unit, marriage is a mere charade and unfaithfulness a matter of course. But let not this one small sadness disguise the fact that for the negroes this is indeed a happy hedonistic life, with ample food, much singing and dancing, regular visits to the physicians, hospitals a-plenty, good housing, healthy labour, and an abundance of friendship.

I have been led to believe that in the past there was some tension between the Africans and the *creoles*. Disputes between these different types of slave were regularly initiated by the *creoles*, who held in contempt those closer to Africa as being the produce of *Guinea-men*. Bonds tighter than family were often struck between the offspring of two men who travelled to these shores in the same bottom, and such bonding would often lead to resentment among the *creole* blacks who had long forgotten, if indeed they had ever known, the true nature of their origins, over and above some loosely imagined fabrications relating to times long since past. These days, now that the acquisition of fresh African slaves is no longer legal, the breeding system has acquired a greater significance than hitherto. I observed a negress who, having enriched my father, held up her new-born child with the words, 'See misses, see! Here nice new nigger me born to bring for work for misses.' And her sentiments are by no means unusual. High status is granted a woman who can bring forth many *creole* children to populate the plantation, and it has not been unknown for a woman to be rewarded for such labour by being granted her freedom. Stella's own *sister* explained to me that she had 'twelve whole children and three half ones', by which she meant miscarriages. And should one chance to hear of a 'one-belly woman', she will be labouring under 'the pleasing punishment which women bear', and is therefore discharged from all severe labour, except of course the terrors and agonies of the labour of child-birth itself, which in these parts is no simple matter.

It is generally the elderly and most obstinately ignorant women who attend the breeders at the time of child-birth. Their tampering has in many instances led to the mother or child or both breathing their last before the mortal nature of the confinement is recognized, and a proper medical attendant can be summoned. Happy is the mother who survives this harpy-trial; her issue is added joyously to the list of the slave population in the plantation-book. But sadly, her joy will not endure beyond a few weeks, for these women are soon pressed again into service and driven afield. I heard complaints from one such bearer who claimed, 'Misses, me have pickaninny two weeks in de sick-house, den out upon the hoe again and we can't strong that way, misses, we can't strong.' On the mothers' return to the fields their progeny are lost to the charge of these self-same midwives. It is only to be expected that before long the pleasures of field-gossip far outweigh the burdens of that weary duty known as *motherhood*. In short, these *mothers* soon prefer their pigs to their own children. To conclude, I sometimes believe that the black woman can produce little *atoms* at will, and when they are barren, it is so only because they are discontented with their circumstances (as a hen will not lay her eggs on board ship). However, the pleasures and benefits that accrue to these breeders lead some dissemblers to insist, for many months more than is generally required to replenish the human race, that they are in 'a state of goodly hope'.

A trait which suggests an inconsistency with the other low characteristics of the negro is the male negro's affection for his mother, irrespective of how cruelly he may have been spurned at birth. Nothing can more provoke a negro to instant enragement and subsequent violence, than a disrespectful remark about his mother, no matter how trifling or inconsequential this remark may appear to be. The male negro son will be diligent in securing the comfort of his mother, be she in sickness or in health. It must be acknowledged that there is some virtue to the negro's loyalty in this respect, and some virtue also in the negro's attitude towards the older members of his ebon community. Old negroes are seldom allowed to live alone or required to perform the duties of cooking. Whether infirm or not, these responsibilities are borne by younger people who will administer to their needs, including attending to their provision grounds in the mountains. They do so in exchange for a trifling return of produce, and all manner of negroes, be they *creole* or African, treat the elderly with respect and kindness, and endeavour to make their old age comfortable.

Our earthly sojourn must terminate in death, and to mark this occasion the negroes have devised many strange and fantastical ceremonies which they perform in their own gardens. If the corpse is that of an adult they consult it as to the manner and location in which it pleases to be interred. Then, bearing the coffined weight of the carcass upon their shoulders, a group of negroes sets out to locate this resting place, each receiving various signals from their long-lost acquaintance, each pulling in different directions, so that it is by no means unusual for the coffin to jump from their shoulders and tumble to the ground while the bearers settle the matter with their fists. Having committed their fellow creatures to the earth, the negroes sit by the mound determined to accompany their friends wherever it may be that they are going on their final journey upon this earth before they commence a new existence.

As the negroes are very superstitious I found it unusual

that they chose to have their dead buried in their gardens, for they fear *jumbys* (ghosts) with a vengeance. These *jumbys* or apparitions are believed to compel the onlooker to follow them, and even run off from the plantation, although it might be more rationally considered that on these occasions the negroes make something of a convenience of their *jumbys*. Apparently the *jumbys* the negroes must truly fear are those of their enemies, and even in death they never suffer their foes to be buried near them. The difference between a benign and a malignant *jumby* is given much consideration. It follows then that the negroes generally believe in a life beyond this world which will involve their return to their own country. However, the decline in sable freight has led to fewer of the negroes having any idea of a country beyond these shores, so that some other place not rooted in reality has long since been substituted for the concept of a *home* country.

It was surprising for me to note how many of those negroes who claimed some memory or association with Africa denied any affection for this link. Whether I was being humoured on account of my alabaster skin I know not, but such conversations often proceeded as follows. *Were you a free man in Africa?* 'Me a Mandingo and dey tek me a Guinea coast to sell to Buckra captain. But me well glad to leave that cruel place, misses, well glad.' *How old were you on your arrival in the West Indies?* 'A big, big man, but me no wan' go back in Africa for they slave me and whip me to death. Whip me, lash me to death, so me like this West Indies truly.' *But what of your friends and family in Africa?* 'Friends and family happy to sell pickaninny to Buckra-man so me no trust them at all. Me go yonder and see England next, me wan' to see English cold.' *Do you know what ice is?* 'Me know, me know, ice is Englishman's water. Me hear so, me wan' go see with these two peepers.'

Perhaps the commonest of all the negro airs that I have given ear to, and one of the very few that I have been able to distinguish as *English*, reflects the rootlessness of these people

who have been torn from their native soil and thrust into the
busy commerce of our civilized world. It is much to be doubted
that they will ever again reclaim a true sense of self. The evidence
before my eyes suggests that such a process will unfold only after
the passage of many decades, perhaps many centuries. It will not
be swift.

If me want for go in a Ebo
Me can't go there!
Since dem tief me from a Guinea
Me can't go there!

If me want for go in a Congo
Me can't go there!
Since dem tief me from my tatter
Me can't go there!

If me want for go in a Baytown,
Me can't go there!
Since massa go in a England,
Me can't go there!

I shall conclude my brief observations with the anecdote of
Caesar, a poor creature who, with his thick, sullen features,
over-hanging eyebrows, and face half covered in hair, gives
a convincing portrayal of *Master Bruin* himself. Sadly, he was
recently stricken with a progressive malady, but I *nursed* him
with particular care and he is almost recovered and returned
to his trade as a carpenter. The poor fellow, so he believes,
cannot sufficiently express his gratitude, and whenever he sees
me, dances about extravagantly, crying, 'God bless you, misses!
Me glad, glad to see you. God bless you!' He will then burst into
a roar of laughter so wild and clamorous that I fear I shall never
accustom myself to its rude excess. The poor fellow's jargon is
beyond me, but I cannot write the salt tears, affecting looks,

and piteous gestures that render it truly pathetic. Suffice to say, this Caesar appears determined to laud me to the skies with his untiring *eloquence*. It seems as though I am to be his eternal heroine, though I did but apply a small poultice to his brow and sit with him on two afternoons.

If treated with care these children are as loyal as any creatures under the sun. They may differ from us in their disregard of marriage vows, and they clearly have difficulty in performing any duty without giving voice to melody, or relaxing without tripping the light fantastic with their toes, but they are in our charge and must be provided for. These days few bottoms arrive, and those which do bear traffic from other islands, with only the occasional ship illegally carrying fresh African stock. It would thus appear that the welcome process of *creolization* is advanced and advancing apace. This being the case, we must be bold enough to take on the responsibility that comes with ownership, and learn to care with even greater dutiful application.

Without rank and order any society, no matter how sophisticated, is doomed to admit the worst kind of anarchy. In this West Indian sphere there is amongst the white people too little attention paid to differences of class. A white skin would appear passport enough to a life of privilege, without due regard to the grade of individuals within the range of that standing. The only exception I have so far observed was the modesty displayed by the book-keeper who first conveyed me here. However, sensible to propriety, he has subsequently maintained his distance. The other men, perhaps because I am a woman, have shown little courtesy in affording the attentions proper to my rank. They converse with me as freely and as openly as they wish. This is barely tolerable amongst the whites, but when I find the blacks hereabouts behaving in the same manner I cannot abide it, and see no reason why I should accommodate myself to the lack of decorum which characterizes this local practice.

Today I arrived at the luncheon table and yet again found Mr Brown's strange and haughty black woman, Christiania, seated opposite me. I ordered her to retire from the table, for I am not accustomed to eating my meal in the company of slaves. Further, I informed this coal-black *ape-woman* that I desired her to put on a serving gown and take up a role among my attendants, male and female, who properly circled the table to wait upon their mistress. On a property belonging to Christian owners, this was her rightful place. Unfortunately, she seemed to display a total lack of concern at my words, and showed no sign of quitting her chair, so I asked her again if she would kindly remove her person in order that I might commence my luncheon. The wench cast on me a look of intense passion that indeed appeared unhinged, her eyes blazing with a malice the source of which I imagined to reside deep in her bosom, springing from some other hurt than that which I had inflicted upon her. Her manner becoming frivolous, she then tossed her head in seeming annoyance. 'Massa say I can eat at table. Why missy not like me?' This, as you might imagine, only served to compound the insult of her presence. That she was asking after me an explanation of my behaviour caused my blood to overheat, and I began to tremble with indignation.

Again, this time in a more uncompromising voice, I ordered her to rise and leave my table. When it became clear that she was set on her stubborn course I turned to the chief butler, a slight-looking fellow greying around the temples who, it must be admitted, appeared at least as outraged as I by this woman's display of intransigence. I ordered this black retainer to escort the negress from my table. He immediately set down his burnished silver platter and approached her, whereupon she began to scream in the most reckless and foul-spoken manner, spitting out words whose meaning I dared not imagine. It proved sufficient to cause the butler to back away. The unfortunate lackey turned to me, pleading for clemency. 'Missy, she too dangerous, altogether too dangerous.' For a third time, now beside myself with fury, I shouted my commands at the black woman, but her lungs were better fitted for the occasion than mine, as she loosed her invective upon me, howling and hurling abuse like some sooty witch from *Macbeth*. At this juncture, I am sorry to admit, my cue was to flee into the sanctuary of my bed-chamber where I concealed both my tear-stained face and my impotent rage.

I had determined to isolate myself in my soft and feminine chamber, uncharacteristic of the Great House, until the merciful day of my departure, which I knew I would welcome much as a prisoner might greet the end of his hated sentence. It was then that I heard a knock upon the door, and the quiet voice of my companion Stella. I drew back the bolt and admitted her to my chamber, whereupon I noted that she seemed equally afflicted by the events that I had recently been compelled to endure. Further, she appeared distressed that she had not been in attendance to offer me support both moral and practical. Quickly I shut in the door and bade her rest in a large basket-chair, while I reclined upon the Holland sheet. 'Missy,' she began, 'Christiania is obeah woman, but massa do like she and that is enough.' Well, this was information too rich for me to comprehend at once, so I asked her to explain.

According to Stella's testimony, the negro belief in *obeah* involves the possession of a variety of strange objects which are used for incantations: cats' ears, the feet of various animals, human hair, fish bones, etc., all of which make their vital contribution to the practice of the magical art. One skilled in the practice of obeah is able to both deliver persons to, and retrieve them from the clutches of, their enemies. Such practitioners hold great sway over their fellow blacks, and they sell medicines and charms in profusion, thus acquiring a status unsurpassed within the community. It would appear that this traffic in charms and remedies is the business of Christiania, which manifestly explained the reluctance of my other slaves to cross the woman, but assuredly did not explain Mr Brown's desire to have her share his table.

Putting aside all modesty, I felt it only proper that I investigate further. I asked if the black Christiania was indeed a slave and the property of my family. 'Yes, missy. She in your service.' *But what is her role on the estate?* 'Missy, she just in the house. She don't have no use as such.' I began to grow impatient. I asked if she was something to Mr Brown, but Stella professed ignorance of what I was suggesting. I informed Stella that I had been sufficiently alert to realize that it is sometimes the custom for white men to retain what they term *housekeepers*. These swarthy dependants elevate their status by prostrating themselves. Stella was vociferous, in defence of whom I am not sure. She spoke against these liaisons with such force that I recalled the proverbial saw that 'the lady doth protest too much'. I did not think that I imagined a conspiracy of black womanhood against white, but I knew that I would find this difficult to prove. Therefore I thought it best to reveal to Stella my awareness of such *amours*, in the hope that she would realize that by speaking frankly, she was unlikely to cause me grief.

Apparently such illicit relationships came about because comparatively few wives journey out to the tropics, and those that do are often distinguished by the meagreness of their conversation with their husbands. As a result concubinage appears to have become universal. I revealed to Stella that I was also aware that the highest position on which a sable damsel could set her sights was to become the mistress of a white man. They seek such unions with planters, overseers, book-keepers, doctors, merchants and lawyers, and when their beauties fail, they seek similar positions for their daughters, knowing that success will assure them of a life of ease and prestige among their own people. This much I have gleaned from my brief perusal of the tawdry newspapers, from conversation, and from a knowledge of human conduct observed not only in these parts but in England also. Naturally, the children of such unions receive the status of the slave mother, unless manumitted by their fathers. They seldom achieve recognition as full heirs, and rarely rise above the skills of the artisan. These hybrid people, who hold themselves above the black, but below the white, abound throughout these island possessions as physical evidence of moral corruption.

All of this I conveyed to Stella in the hope that she might be persuaded to share her knowledge with me, but I succeeded only in arousing her ire. It appeared that she took offence at the manner in which I portrayed the ambitions of black womanhood, but she manifested her rage not by overt onslaught, but by covert smouldering. I asked her if it were not true that young black wenches are inclined to lay themselves out for white lovers, and hence bring forth a spurious and degenerate breed, neither fit for the field nor for any work that the true-bred negro would relish. She would not answer. I asked her if it was not entirely understandable that such women would become licentious and insolent past all bearing because of their privileged position? Again, she would say nothing in response. I informed her that I have even heard intelligence that if a mulatto child threatens to interrupt a black woman's pleasure, or become a troublesome heir, there are certain herbs and medicines, including the juice of the cassava plant, which seldom fail to free the mother from this inconvenience. At this point Stella seemed ready to quit my chamber. Her insolence fired me, and I resolved to cast my accusatory stone where it properly belonged. I demanded that Stella immediately conduct me to Mr Brown. At this Stella protested that it was the height of the afternoon, and that I should not be exposed to the vertical rays from on high, but I insisted. The arrogance of the inky wench, who had dared publicly to preside at my table, still burned within me. I wished to quiz Mr Brown as to her status.

Indeed the sun was high. I had but stepped ten paces from the Great House before I knew that I ought not to be so exposed.

Stella was correct. We were attended by Hazard and Androcles, two inferior lackeys who carried our parasols and sauntered along with an air which belongs to creatures unfettered by those responsibilities which are the familiar burden of rational humanity. Stella carried herself with comical self-assurance, quite as if she were a white. I can remember little of the walk to the fields, where according to *fair* Stella our Mr Brown was supervising his drivers, but I do recall that on more than one occasion I felt sure that I should expire before we reached our destination. Inwardly I cursed myself for even attempting such a journey, but after what seemed an eternity Stella finally pointed out Mr Brown. As we approached, a flight of birds rose in the air and cast a shadow like that of a cloud, causing the sun to darken for a few seconds. I found new resolution, and stormed ingloriously across the field, leaving instructions that Stella was not to follow.

The slaves ceased their Sisyphean labours and inclined their heads towards the wild Englishwoman charging across the denuded cane-piece. Noticing this, Mr Brown understood that something was amiss. He too turned and watched, waiting, hands upon hips and whip in hand, for my approach. 'Mr Brown,' I demanded, 'what is the meaning of this black woman sharing my dining table?' Mr Brown stared at me as though I had finally taken leave of my senses in this inhospitable climate. 'I will not tolerate such a vile and offensive perversion of good taste,' I cried. 'I demand your assurance that she will never again be allowed to disgrace my table.' Mr Brown raised a hand to block the sun from his face. He seemed rather confused by my performance, and he nodded as though uncertain of why he was doing so. For some time we stood, toe to toe, two solitary white people under the powerful sun, casting off our garments of white decorum before the black hordes, each vying for supremacy over the other.

I played my final card. 'Mr Brown, if you do not display more consideration for my position, immediately upon my return

I shall have you replaced.' Mr Brown, with no discernible movement of his body, and certainly without taking his eyes from my face, called to his trustee, Fox. He ordered this black man to bear me back to the Great House. Fox, a somewhat docile but evidently sturdy negro, positioned himself before me. I repeated my threat, but Mr Brown simply uttered the word 'Fox', at which point the nigger laid his black hands upon my body, at which I screamed and felt my stomach turn in revulsion, at which its contents emptied upon the ground. Despite the heat of the day, I felt a cold shudder through my body, and I tried desperately to keep back a sob of distress. Thereafter, I have to confess that my memory remains blank until I regained consciousness in the coolness of my chamber with my Stella in attendance on me.

I judged from the sounds of nature without, and the darkness within, that the later hours of the evening were upon us. I was pleased to see the loyal Stella hover over me with concern writ large and bold across her sooty face. How far she has come in matching the loyalty of the dearly departed Isabella! Although sadly lacking the natural advantages of my former companion, and incapable of mastering even the most elementary intellectual science of the alphabet, my sable companion has virtue still. Her smiling ebon face and broadly grinning lips, which display to good advantage her two rows of ivory, offer a greeting that has helped make tolerable my sojourn on this small island in the Americas. I have been thinking seriously of taking her back with me to England, but my fear is that she may be mocked as an exotic, as are the other blacks who congregate about the parish of St Giles and in divers parts of our kingdom. However, when the time is ripe I will suggest to her that she might wish to meet with her master in his own country, the prospect of which, I am sure, will delight her. I cannot believe that any West Indian negro would spurn the opportunity of serving their master a quart of ale and a tossed tea-cake on a wintry English night.

On my regaining fuller awareness, my first enquiry of Stella brought forth the much feared response. Indeed there was much to regret. It would appear that Fox carried me bodily back to the Great House, and Stella has sat with me since. Stella informed me that Mr McDonald was summoned to attend, and that having done so he has stayed on in the hope that he might be present once I had recovered my senses. I instructed Stella to send him away, which she proceeded to do. She returned within the minute, a light smile etched upon her sable countenance. It seems that she is no longer fond of our physician, having detected a certain warmth in his passions towards me which she is happy to see dowsed by my new coolness. Stella served me yet another glass of the medicinal *sangaree* and began to inform me of Mr Brown's concern for my condition. I said nothing, thus giving her the chance to release from within whatever was troubling her mind. She paused, and then seized the opportunity. Stella suggested that Mr Brown is in a difficult situation, having neither wife, nor children, and he has been upon this plantation for many years, first as book-keeper, lately as assistant, and now as overseer and manager. I let her continue. Stella added that nobody knows the plantation as Mr Brown does and that although he is hard, and perhaps a little coarse and unconventional, he is generally known to be a fair man, the implication behind the black woman's peroration being that my conduct had been somehow improper to interfere in his smooth running of the estate. I sighed. What this sooty illiterate could never hope to understand is that by coming to visit I was far exceeding the duties that most proprietors set for themselves. And without a visit, I could never have discovered that my father's deputed authority was being abused and his property, including dear Stella, exploited. I held my tongue and let her continue. Her final words on the subject were poignant, if somewhat offensive, although I took it that they were not meant to be interpreted as being disrespectful. 'Here is no place for missy. Missy have a better life in she own country.' I smiled at Stella, even as I felt my eyelids grow heavy with sleep's ever-increasing burden. So missy have a better life in her own country? Perhaps Stella thinks that missy ought to hurry back to Mr Thomas Lockwood? Perhaps Stella thinks missy is jealous of Christiania and her obeah? Who knows what she thinks. I asked Stella to sit with me, worried as I was that my dreams might become over-populated with dark incubae. She turned down the light, folded her hands into a comfortable bundle, and dropped them into her dark lap. I knew she would not desert me, not this evening.

This past week has marked a profound change in the heart and soul of Mr Brown. I can only assume that his gentler aspect has made an appearance as a result of guilt, but whatever it is that has provoked this miraculous improvement in his behaviour I am truly grateful for this reformed state of affairs. It serves to render the remaining few weeks of my sojourn on this West Indian island a little more tolerable, a factor of considerable import for one with a constitution as feeble as mine. Furthermore, the intemperate vehemence of my entreaties seems to have borne fruit. I am happy to report that not only does *gentle* Mr Brown appear to have forbidden the black Christiania to sit at the dining table, he seems to have confined her and her primitive obeah to the negro village. The effect upon the household slaves has been truly miraculous, for without the vulture presence of this negress casting a shadow over their persons they have all adopted a sunnier aspect. Mr Brown has taken to dressing for dinner. That he has a wardrobe that admits of fashion startled the breath from my body. True, he sports no more than a jacket and a fresh pair of breeches, but they are clean. I assume that by donning these clothes he intends to offer up some sign that he is at least aware of the social and liberal arts, the same arts with which one could be forgiven for having assumed he lacked all acquaintance.

Dinners upon Father's estate have always been lavish, yet these days they seem, if anything, to have increased in grandeur.

Mr Brown and I share a now familiar bountiful supper. The daily feast offers kid, lamb, poultry, pork and a variety of fish. I have adjusted myself to tolerate poorly dressed meat served without butter, unless a shipment from Ireland or England happens to have been freshly landed (although fresh it is unlikely to be after such a voyage). As usual the turtle forms the centre-piece of these dinners, but increasingly crab and lobster are being offered up for our delight. The odour of the slaves who attend us is also somewhat improved. The swarms of fleas that commonly cohabit with our sable dependants appear to have taken up residence elsewhere. However, it is still a problem to persuade the blacks to wear shoes upon their feet. Mr Brown has confided to me that the negro feels more of a chattel when shod than he does when decked in chains, so greatly does he detest the footwear we take for granted. This preference in going barefoot also accounts for the lameness preponderant among the negroes, a consequence of infection by the *chegoe*.

The dessert is generally superior to the main course, the finest fruits being provided in abundance. Mr Brown took the trouble to explain to me the mysteries of two fruits which regularly grace our table. Apparently the *shaddock* contains thirty-two seeds, two of which will reproduce the fruit, but it is impossible to distinguish which two. The rest will between them yield some sweet oranges, some bitter, and some will bring forth forbidden fruit. In short, all varieties of orange are likely progeny of the shaddock, though no flavour is much alike. It is not until the trees start to bear that one is able to detect success or failure, for until this blessing the trees appear much the same. However, the seeds that happily reproduce the shaddock, even if taken from an exceptionally fine specimen, may bear only tolerable, or inferior fruit, some of which is scarcely edible. The mystery of the *mango* is no less baffling. Mr Brown tells me that the fruit of no two trees is the same, and that the seeds of the finest mango, though carefully sown and cultivated, seldom result in fruit comparable to the parent stock. At its best the mango is the queen fruit of the islands; at worst its flavour resembles turpentine and sugar. I enquired as to the possibility of returning to England bearing some seeds from which I might attempt to cultivate this exotic plant in my own little piece of England, but it seems I am likely to be disappointed.

Remarkably enough our exchanges have often continued until late in the evening, when we have sat upon the piazza sipping at dishes of tea, trying hard to ignore the mosquito-gentry who pay us close attention, especially after dusk. We are particularly careful to ensure that our conversation remains impersonal, neither of us wishing to spoil this new companionship. So Mr Brown speaks principally with me of West Indian affairs. In turn I explain, as best I can, what is afoot in England, which country, I am sad to learn, Mr Brown has not visited for some twenty or more years. His interest in England appears to be merely polite, and I think one might safely assume that he will bequeath his body to West Indian soil, among the people he seems to understand so well. As to the nature of the trade he is engaged in, I doubt if there is anybody who knows more than Mr Brown about the business of squeezing profit from a moderately sized plantation in the tropical zone. On this point everyone, from Stella to Mr McDonald, agrees. When I displayed interest in the technical procedures employed in cultivation of the cane, Mr Brown offered to escort me around the property, provided our tour began early the next morning. He also promised to show me the principal scenes of life on a sugar plantation.

Without *King Sugar* none would be here, neither black nor white. The method of sugar-cane production, upon which all tropical wealth depends, formed the elementary lesson of my day with Mr Brown. First, explained my master, the ripe canes are cut in the field and brought in bundles to the sugar mill, where the cleanest of the black women are employed to deliver the canes into the machines for grinding, while a solitary black woman draws them out at the other end once the juice has been extracted. She then throws the emaciated cane through an opening in the floor, where a pack of negroes is employed in bundling up this *trash* for use as fuel. The precious cane-juice gushes out of the grinding machine through a wooden gutter, and becomes quite white with foam. It streams into the boiling house, and enters a siphon where it is heated by the boiler. It is slaked with lime to encourage it to granulate. The scum rises to the top, while the purer and more fluid juice flows through another gutter into a second siphon or copper. When little but the scum on the surface remains, the gutter communicating with the first copper is blocked off. The remaining waste travels through a final gutter, which conveys it to the distillery. Here this solution is mixed with molasses or treacle to become rum.

The pure juice in the second copper is then fed back into the first, and then on into two more, each time more scum being removed from the surface with a copper skimmer pierced with holes. This enables the fresh juice to flow back into the coppers. When free from impurities, the juice is ladled into coolers where it is left to granulate. Sugar is formed in the curing house. As the sugar settles, the part of it that is too poor in quality or too liquid to granulate is allowed to drip off from the casks into vessels placed beneath them. These drippings form the molasses, which is taken into the distillery and mixed with the coarser scum to make rum, after two distillations. The first distillation produces only 'low wine'. Under the guidance of Mr Brown I was able to observe all the tools, utensils and instruments employed in this industry, but it not being the season I was unable to see the process in full operation. However, Mr Brown's explanation was so thorough that not only do I feel confident that I might explain the mysteries of this process to any stranger, but I am persuaded that I must myself have observed it in action!

The empty canes that form the trash are most commonly utilized as fuel. However, some canes are used for fodder or as thatching. The *cane-tops* are cut off and replanted in order to cultivate fresh growths. There is another method employed if one wishes to conserve time. It seems that after the original growths have been cut their roots throw up suckers, which mature to become canes. These are known as *ratoons*. They are much inferior in juice to the planted canes, but require less weeding and spare the negroes the only laborious part of the business of sugar-making, the excavation of holes for planting; however, an acre of *ratoons* will produce only one hogshead of sugar, while an acre of fresh plants will produce two. But the *ratoons* save time, effort and expense, and a thoroughgoing planter can cultivate five acres of *ratoons* in the time it will take him to cultivate one acre of plants. However, nature is not to be outdone and Mr Brown, with some regret, informed me that after four or five crops of *ratoons* this cyclical process is utterly exhausted and one is obliged to plant fresh *cane-tops*. That it was possible for one to extract even so much seemed to me one of nature's more generous bargains. Chief among accidents and injuries is burning, usually caused by drunken negroes stepping into the siphons in the boiling-houses. If the fire has not long been kindled the limb can generally be rescued, but sometimes there is little one can do, and the doctor is forced to resort to amputation, after which neither replanting nor *ratoon* will restore the limb.

With Mr Brown I walked the lush pastures of the estate, from time to time being provided the facility to refresh myself with water. The cisterns in which the water for *family-use* is kept are very well-calculated to preserve the water cool and fresh for some time. What is used for drinking, and supplies the table, passes through a filtering stone into a lead and marble reservoir, which causes it to become more lucid and pure than any water I have ever seen. The reservoir is placed in a shaded corner to preserve the chill, and the water is presented by a slave. The negro offers the water in a coconut shell ornamented with silver, and attached to the end of a hickory handle. This is to prevent the breath of the swarthy bondsman contaminating the purity of the water. Mr Brown was always generous with explanations of any questions I might ask, and ready to label a tree or shrub whose colour or particular grace might attract my eye. However, when I ventured upon more controversial ground, that one might argue is at the heart of the matter, namely slavery, my guide seemed somewhat reluctant to discuss the *institution*. It would appear that Mr Brown feels that the ethical and moral questions raised by this mode of profit are matters on which I am not yet qualified to engage. Perhaps he objects to discussing such matters with a woman? It is difficult for me to tell. He did, however, suggest that the proposal to substitute animal for black labour arose from pure ignorance. Mr Brown informed me that on many plantations oxen ploughs and other farming implements had been purchased, but through obstinacy and ignorance the negroes simply broke plough after plough and ruined one beast after another. All such attempts have had to be abandoned, for once broken, the cast-iron ploughs cannot be repaired for lack of artisan skills. As for the livestock, efforts to shelter them from heat and rain have proved worthless. Furthermore, the negroes did not seem to understand that the labouring cattle were not as hardy as they, and could not effectively be driven from sun-up to sun-down. Shortly after their arrival the livestock inevitably began to decline, their blood was converted into urine, and expiration soon followed. This, it would appear, constituted the sum total of Mr Brown's case for the continuation of the institution of slavery. In short, if negroes do not labour, then who will? After all, according to my instructor, white men and animals are unsuited to this form of drudgery.

I have spent the greater part of the last few days in thoughtful consideration of the *institution*. In this frame of mind I have written yet again to Father informing him that upon my return I would wish to make a small lecture tour. A discourse upon my changing fortunes and adventurous travel upon the Atlantic

Ocean, and beyond, upon its further shores. This might be of interest to some of the ladies' associations founded by the wives of these new men of industry, especially if my reflections are supported by my immediate experience. When I left these shores I promised Father that I would endure the tropic heat with an open mind as to the merits of the trade in and employment of slaves, and this I have tried to do. But this tired system is lurching towards an end, a fact which it would be foolish to deny. Overworking of the land, absenteeism on the part of those like Father (who fail to recognize that this business of sugar-planting requires the full attention of those who engage in it), the innate menace of this zone, the loss of trade with the newly independent states in America, the afflictions of war in Europe, and, as I observed under the tutelage of Mr Brown, the sad inefficiency of production, all these ills have contributed to the unpropitious future of the West Indian sugar industry. Soon the English must abandon this seeming paradise. Father has connections enough to aid me in a small lecture tour, and I have also suggested that such a tour might help to defer the expense of his sending me upon this journey. I might even compose a short pamphlet framed as a reply to the lobby who, without any knowledge of life in these climes, would seek to have us believe that slavery is nothing more than an abominable evil.

Such untravelled *thinkers* do not comprehend the base condition of the negro. Nor do they appreciate the helplessness of the white man in his efforts to preserve some scrap of moral decency in the face of so much provocation and temptation. We all hope to welcome the day when liberty shall rule over an ample domain, but at present the white man's unfitness for long toil under the rays of a vertical sun would appear to go some way to justify his colonial employment of negro slaves, whose bodies are better suited to labour in tropical heat. To speak with sentiment merely of the sale and purchase of such people without *full* consideration of the universal economic facts

is plain foolishness. This being the case, I have also informed
Father that I shall continue to reside on this plantation for a
further three months, during which time I shall have completed
the notes for both my pamphlet and my lecture tour. I advised
Mr Brown of my decision, to which he merely nodded as
though the news were of no consequence to him. After all, I
do not believe for one minute that he is under any illusion as to
where my loyalties lie: in other words, that is, with my father,
his employer and his master. What else could he display but
resignation? He was, of course, obliged to remain silent with
regard to any fears he might harbour that my writings might
comment adversely upon his conduct.

Late last night, having no doubt been informed by Stella of
my extended residence, the negroes took it into their heads to
pay me a compliment of an extremely inconvenient nature. In
order to display their pleasure at my continued sojourn among
them, they thought it proper to treat me to a nocturnal serenade.
Accordingly, a large body of well-dressed negroes arrived under
my window about midnight, accompanied by drums, rattles,
and a full orchestra of such unlikely instruments. Thereafter,
there appeared to me a congregation of black limbs tumbling
and leaping and seemingly determined to pass the whole night
singing and dancing beneath my balcony. From their lungs
bellowed forth stentorian snatches of Bacchanalian songs, and
their unseemly laughter disturbed the still night air. Their
fiddlers, cognizant of neither sharps nor flats, embraced with
enthusiasm their old friend *discord*, while those who danced
were unable to prolong their individual exertions above a
minute or two; nevertheless, this sufficed to distil an abundance
of perspiration. Such a vulgar, yet dextrous, set of antics never
came into the brain, or out of the limbs, of anything but a *son
of Ham* enjoying his jubilee. After an hour of this Dionysiac
abomination, I instructed Stella to inform them that I had
long since retired and that they should withdraw promptly
to their village. This she did, and then presented herself once

more, whereupon she began to address me, her countenance displaying a degree of concern which approached severity.

Dear Stella. Things between us have not been easy of late. I suspect that she is a shade jealous of the attention that Mr Brown has recently bestowed upon me. I suspect also that he has exchanged fewer words with her than was the case before my arrival. Jealousy being the transitory emotion that it is, I am sure that this difficulty will soon pass, and before long a familiar sweet smile will once more be embellishing her features so that despite their dusky tint they might reassume the appearances of both gentleness and refinement. There has been no sign of Christiania for some while, and Stella and I are once again the dominant females of the household. Dear Stella, she seemed delighted to hear that I would be prolonging my visit, and I am sure that the emotions she displayed were no mere show of theatrical skill. We two sat together until all the negroes had ceased their noisy revelry and returned to their lairs and nests. What we in England call autumn is now upon us. Stella, seemingly both exhausted and preoccupied with her own cogitations, informed me that we were entering the time of the rainy season, with its occasional hurricane. Then she closed her eyes.

The sultriness began to give way to more windy weather, promising a most boisterous and tempestuous night. A sudden flurry swelled into a gale, the thunder began to peal most awfully, and the lightning flashed its fearful fires. The dark clouds laboured to rest upon the mountains, and the wind called mournfully among the trees. As the air became chill, the mercury fell, and the shuttered casements of heaven opened wide. And then, as suddenly as the skies opened, they closed up again. I knew from past experience that one consequence of such rain is that in the morning animal life of all kinds will be crowding for space. The ground will be discovered to be littered with lizards, centipedes and cockroaches, all of whom will be present in platoons, under cushions, behind bookshelves, lurking in the most unlikely places. One has to learn not to fear these ugly black creepers and crawlers; there are negro boys a-plenty to crush each noisome creature the moment it invades one's life. There is no stemming the invasion. The creatures are sent to try us, but we must not relax our patient self-defence.

Disconcertingly, the emotion of fear is becoming increasingly familiar to me. These past nights the sensation has seized me again, causing me to recollect the prior occasion on which I felt such trepidation. After the death of Isabella at sea, the demon made his last assault. As these alarms continued to threaten me in my impotence, I feared that I should soon be reunited with my dead companion. And now this devilish fear has reasserted its power, but this time I find myself adrift, not on threatening waves, but upon an ocean of negroes who care little for my fears. Outside my window, I began to discern nocturnal scratching noises. At first I was too frightened to properly investigate, in fear that some strange beast might be waiting for an opportunity to assault and devour me body and soul. Eventually, on the third night, I pulled back a corner of the blind and peered into the darkness, whereupon I observed the re-entry into the drama of my life of the arrogant black wench, Christiania. Squatting down on her hams, she appeared to be scratching at the dirt, to what purpose I knew not. Furthermore, she was uttering sinister sounds which I did not wish to hear repeated throughout the night. I thought it best not to approach the half-witted creature directly, especially as I was sure that she was unaware of being observed by me. So I called to Stella, directed her attention to the origin of these noises, and instructed her to drive away the crazy woman. Before Stella could jabber a reply, I read the reluctance in her sooty countenance. I have hitherto observed that amongst the other blacks, there is a deep fear of this foolish Christiania, a fear which has its origins in this obeah that they pay so much attention to, about which I have gleaned further information. This dark practice was brought by the negroes from Africa, where open and devoted worship of the devil is still encouraged, and temples erected in his honour. The doctors and professors of this obeah are known to have entered into a league with Satan, and with his aid are able to seal the doom of all those who offend them. A fear of the sudden afflictions that this obeah is irrationally believed to call forth strikes terror in the woolly negro head piece. The symptoms include the loss of appetite, day-long fretting and brooding, a perverse desire to consume what is patently indigestible, a heavy listlessness, gross swelling of the extremities, and in due course, an inexplicable death. Clearly Stella, in common with the other plantation slaves, feared that such marvellous powers would be visited upon her person, should she choose to incur the anger of this Christiania. Accordingly, Stella did not venture an inch to carry out any instructions to send Christiania on her way, so I deemed it proper to repeat the order more forcibly. You hear these noises, I insisted, and asked, What is she doing down there upon her knees? Stella pleaded ignorance, and backed hesitantly from my chamber. I let close an hour pass before summoning her again. The noise was growing increasingly frightful, and I demanded of Stella what was signalled by this woman's persistent animal scrabblings and croakings beneath my window. At this the poor woman burst into tears and confessed that, 'Massa say we no talk with Christiania. Massa say we leave she be.' This really was becoming quite intolerable!

As chance would have it, Mr Brown was away visiting a plantation on our sister-island, to intercede in a dispute between the slave stock and an overseer. Apparently on some islands this is a common way of settling feuds, by calling in an overseer or agent from a distant estate to adjudicate. One imagines that such decisions would seldom be passed in favour of the blacks, for the whites must surely be required to merely venture a personal preference and encourage a chorus of assent. However, the negroes have little choice but to endure and comply with the system. The critical point was that Mr Brown would not be returning for at least another three to four days, and I could see no manner in which I might pass the time, and retain a sound grip on my sanity, while Christiania persisted in this noisy charade. I instructed Stella, making it clear to her that I was in no way sympathetic to her imprudent distress, to bring before me the book-keeper who first escorted me up to the estate, for I knew that his duty was to deputise for Mr Brown during his absence. Stella stared lugubriously at the space between her splayed feet. Then she remarked upon the lateness of the hour, presumably unsure as to the propriety of a woman visiting a man's chambers in such circumstances. I responded with some spirit, pointing out that the greater impropriety was for a woman attired in rags to be crawling and whining like a dog in the filth, making noises as if she were communing with the devil himself. Upon this, Stella's face fell into the expression of a melancholy ape, and she took a dejected leave of me.

Within the half-hour the book-keeper arrived, ushered into my bed-chamber by a recalcitrant Stella. From the creased wrinkles upon his face, and the heaviness of his lids, I took it that he had been aroused from sleep. From the smell of rum on his breath I could easily ascertain what form of nightcap had been employed to induce such a slumber. In the few months since our introduction, this man seemed to have hurried past the meridian of life and adopted both a round and florid face, and an increasingly bowed and bent bodily form. Although age had tinged his severely barbered hair with grey, and presumably encouraged him to dress with what might at best be described as graceful negligence, time had not succeeded wholly in driving the brightness from his eyes or depressing his shrewdly alert, but nonetheless properly respectful manner. I began to complain, omitting to mention the essential facts, wrongly assuming that Stella would have related these to him. Apparently not. He looked quizzical, and I realized that I should have to begin afresh. But there was, in fact, little required to explain, for the negress ventured anew to utter her beastly noises, and I had only to lead the book-keeper to the window and invite him to view her conduct. He seemed not in the least surprised and asked how he might help. At this juncture I near-lost my patience. You might ask her to leave forthwith and afford me the opportunity to enjoy a little sleep, I suggested. Somewhat embarrassed, the book-keeper informed me that Mr Brown would not tolerate anyone to disturb the woman. He believed that this was on account of her knowledge of the magical arts. Having successfully avoided a direct confrontation with either myself or the black Christiania, our book-keeper then outlined emergency plans for a negro to be immediately stationed outside my room, so that, should there be any intrusive assaults, or magical manifestations, I would simply need to call out and my sable saviour would rush in to protect me. In the fatigued state that I found myself in, I acquiesced to this curious proposal, and the book-keeper took a relieved leave. His scheme appeared much superior to a night of solitude in my chamber, and certainly preferable to the fear-stricken company of Stella. At least a slave outside, and Stella inside, would render some support to my failing spirit.

I opened the door a few inches so I might gain a sight of my negro sentinel. To my astonishment I recognized the negro as Cambridge, the aged slave who had previously had some disagreement with Mr Brown, a debate which had resulted in his being quite tremendously lashed with the cattle-whip. Mr Brown had laid *sambo* down with a flogging whose severity had, according to Stella, obliged the proud black to go to the pond and wash off the blood for many an hour. My dark sentry looked up at me, and I noted that I appeared to have disturbed him in the most unlikely act of studying the Bible. I asked if this was his common form of recreation, to which he replied in highly fanciful English, that indeed it was. You might imagine my surprise when he then broached the conversational lead and enquired after my family origins, and my opinions pertaining to slavery. I properly declined to share these with him, instead counter-quizzing with enquiries as to the origins of his knowledge. At this a broad grin spread over his face, as though I had fallen into some trap of his setting. Indeed, so disturbing was the negro's confident gleam, that I quickly closed in the door, for I feared this negro was truly ignorant of the correct degree of deference that a lady might reasonably expect from a base slave.

Hardly had I settled down into these new circumstances, when there came a light, and a knocking upon the door. Never, outside the performance of one of Shakespeare's plays, had I been subjected to so much drama, counter-drama, indeed melodrama, in such a short space of time. Stella roused herself from the rocker in which she reclined, and cracked the door a little. I heard the voice of Mr McDonald and called to Stella to allow him admittance. He quickly apologized for the late hour, but informed me that a concerned book-keeper had earlier this same evening communicated to him that there was something amiss at the Great House. It appeared that Mr McDonald had taken it upon himself to accompany the sooty messenger back to our plantation in case he should need to pronounce judgement upon some person. I sat up in bed and ordered Stella to fetch some hermitage for the doctor. I then invited him to take up the seat that Stella had vacated, and above the noise of the black woman without I related to him the tales of the evening.

The chapter which seemed to cause him the most anxiety was that which involved stationing the negro male outside my bed-chamber. The impropriety of this new situation had not struck me, my principal concern being for my own safety. But I asked the attentive Mr McDonald whether, were I to dismiss the black, he in turn would be prepared to sit all night outside my chamber. To this Mr McDonald made reply which would have persuaded me that his true profession was lawyer rather than physician. He claimed to have extensive knowledge of the black Christiania, and vigorously assured me that I should expect no danger from this quarter. Stella's presence, he went on, would be security enough. There was, of course, no direct response to my question as to whether or not he would choose to exchange places with the negro sentinel, but I espied clearly the deepest hectic rush to colour the face of the good doctor when I presented him the opportunity to pass the night on my bed-chamber doorstep. However, I virtuously resisted the temptation to tease him further.

Stella returned, and when Mr McDonald had finished his drink he stood up from the rocker. He remarked that the noise seemed somewhat to have abated, but then he continued, having apparently thought of a way in which it might be made to cease altogether. Addressing Stella, he enquired whether the vast negro on sentry duty had some influence with Christiania. In vain Stella attempted to feign indifference, but it was as clear as the blackness of her face that she knew the negro possessed considerable influence. Mr McDonald turned and addressed me. 'If anybody can persuade the negress to depart I think it will be your black sentinel, for he fears nobody and is afforded great respect by the body of slaves.' With this information delivered, Mr McDonald dispatched a sullen Stella to make it known to her dark *brother* what was required of him. I asked the doctor why it was that such a man should come to be beaten so severely by Mr Brown, who otherwise seems a just enough fellow in his attitude and conduct towards the stock. To this Mr McDonald made no answer, except to observe that when two strong wills cross one must expect trouble. I mused upon his words, and then realized that the wolfish noises had ceased. At last I could discern the sounds of nature unobscured by the scratchings of lunacy. I permitted a smile to cross my face and thanked Mr McDonald. At this moment Stella returned. Mr McDonald prepared to take his leave, and as I continued to thank him most properly he informed me that it was neither he nor Stella I should thank, but the giant negro. I asked Stella if the woman had truly ceased her infernal scratching, and I received an affirmative answer. 'Cambridge tell she to stop and so she stop. Is so it do be.' Mr McDonald, clearly pleased with himself, and imagining that he had performed some sterling service on my behalf, bade my person a flourishing farewell and left Stella and myself, and the night, to ourselves.

After this dramatic exercise I certainly did not wish immediately to retire, so I instructed Stella to fetch the chessmen from the central hall, which she did reluctantly, dragging her fatigue behind her. I continued in my pointless quest to acquaint her with this game, but alas she has neither the intelligence even dimly to comprehend the rules, nor the guile even to pretend to possess some notion of its strategies. So time drifted on until poor Stella could no longer feign interest, and eventually she left me exhausted to my tropical night, the bland whisperings of the wind, and the sounds of distant thunder. I feared a storm was due to break, and so in this state of trepidation I passed a restless and wearisome night. However, when morning arrived, and *Master Sol* rose in the east flaunting his majestic splendour, my heart swelled with gratitude towards God who had offered His merciful protection. Through the open window of my chamber poured a warm flood of sunshine chequering the floor. A sweet breeze, as gentle as an infant's breath, soothed me with its cooling air. This was truly a divine display of God's blessing, and I now felt able to relax and submit to the heavenly convenience of peaceful sleep.

Today I was in a complimentary strain and inclined to be a little more jocose than is common. I summoned Mr Rogers in order than I might learn more about this obeah. I wished also to have a decent companion in the absence of Mr Brown, and one with whom I might converse without having to endure the enervating yawn and drawl of the negro accent. We lunched on a light but festive board whose chief delight were fruits of every description, including the succulent pine-apple, the watery melon, the sweet-smelling guava, and the luscious jelly coconut. For those of us who are inclined to take on more flesh than is considered graceful, it proved something of a trial, though pleasantly so. Soon after our conclusion the board was cleared, though a little light wine sparkled in the crystal chalice. I suggested that we two retire to the piazza, where I sported an umbrella to prevent the sun from scorching my head. I drew Mr Rogers's attention to the distant idling skiffs of the fishermen dancing upon the buoyant blue waters, the dark boatmen mastering the *finny race* in silence, but Mr Rogers seemed entirely uninterested in my observations. Really, there is little I can relate of our conversation, for Mr Rogers is truly a most reticent and private man. The longer he lingered, the more he gave me confirmation of Mr McDonald's deceit, when he attempted to persuade me that Mr Rogers had secret designs upon my person. I doubt very much if Mr Rogers has ever had such designs, secret or otherwise, upon any woman in his life. I am tempted to describe him as a fish out of water, but this would not be altogether accurate, for it would be difficult to imagine waters in which Mr Rogers might comfortably swim. I enquired after a small monument for Isabella, and he replied casually that he would investigate. Perhaps, he suggested, a plaque in the cemetery, but he declared in a fashion slightly less indifferent that now my health was restored, and my stay extended, I must make an effort to come and visit his church of St George's in the heart of Baytown. Such monuments as the one I was suggesting for Isabella, he said, were usually paid for by public subscription, for the populace would know the person concerned, but in the case of my beloved Isabella, Mr Rogers was at pains to instruct me that the expense would be mine alone.

As for information about obeah, he was hardly helpful, seemingly knowing less than I had already discovered. To his mind it was simply a dark African mystery, and there was little more to say on the matter. It appeared to be the devil's work, in direct opposition to the heavenly goals towards which Mr Rogers had set his face. These were divinely inspired reformation and holy absolution for the planters, overseers, book-keepers and merchants, all of whom he saw as tainted creatures in this tropical paradise abundant in Edenic temptations. I stifled yawn after yawn as I endured this most tedious of afternoons. On the question of slavery (I was thinking now of my pamphlet and lecture tour) Mr Rogers was predictably dull. After all, I wished to go beyond the commonplace memoirs of previous travellers, who, finding nought worthy of record but the most bizarre features of this tropical life, settle complacently to offer their dumb and helpless audience little more than flimsy defences of the system. My purpose being more ambitious, the pious opinions of Mr Rogers proved inconsequential to me.

It was, he claimed, the job of the white man to look after the children in his care, and the white man would do so in a better manner if he were closer to God. It was not the job of the Church to interfere in politics or economics. As to the education of slaves in matters spiritual, there were some missionaries who had attempted such a course, but Mr Rogers was nervous that this might encourage over-bold negro conduct, even insurrection. These spiritually educated negroes would suddenly require themselves to be addressed as Paul, and John, even Jesus, and view themselves as equal with the white man in the eyes of the Lord. My companion of the cloth went further, and insisted that nothing but the inflexible maintenance of the moral and spiritual superiority of the whites could possibly keep in subjection the physical superiority of the blacks. He insisted that should the negroes become as well-informed as the whites, and should thoughts be implanted, the like of which have never before visited their wool-thatched brains, then the combined forces of the militia and the navy would not be able to keep in check rebellion against their *natural* condition of servitude. Clearly Mr Rogers was a man who would have been happier in an earlier and less enlightened century, for according to him heathenism and devilry seemed destined to sit more firmly upon their black shoulders than the sins of Eden upon the shoulders of white men, and herein lay the true length of his submission.

When Mr Rogers again visited the subject of obeah, this time in fuller detail, he once more informed me that this practice was nothing less than a primitive belief in witchcraft which operated upon the negroes to produce death. He claimed that there was not a single West Indian estate where one or more professors of this obeah do not practise their heathen craft, but he maintained that it is very difficult for the white man to identify these devilish emissaries. However, our churchman soon grew weary of this obeah and returned again to his now familiar sermon. He saved his greatest ire for those injudicious missionary preachers who admitted a few black slaves to sit by night under their roofs and receive the Methodist gospel. From a small beginning this society appears to be spreading far and wide, boasting a vast increase of converts to its *Ebeneezer Chapel*. According to Mr Rogers, these Methodists admit every variety of shade from the ruddy son of the fair fields of England, to the *jettiest* offspring of Africa's black jungles. And so Mr Rogers continued with his homily until I longed for the company of Stella, with or without her chessmen.

My mind began to drift to heavier matters, for on this same day a letter had arrived from England, the first I have received since my sojourn began. Clearly, Father had written in some haste, assuming that I would soon be preparing for my return. The nature of his anxiety concerns Mr Wilson, from whom it appears he has received a letter in which Mr Wilson claims that mutiny has occurred and he has been forcibly ousted and banished to a neighbouring island. What Father would like me to acquire is a statement of explanation from Mr Brown, whose continued position at the head of the plantation does not appear to grate unduly on Father's sensibilities. It seems that he simply desires to give audience to Mr Brown's version of events before deciding on a course of action. There was little else in the short communiqué, aside from his wishing me a safe and speedy return to England. No news of England. None of Mr Thomas Lockwood. None of himself, although one might imagine there to be little of interest to Father beyond his new gambling debts. As to my oft-delivered plea that he make the effort to come and visit his own estate, Father studiously avoids any mention of this in his letter, presumably feeling that my presence here has absolved him of this responsibility. I doubt if he has revised his opinions on this subject, but I will raise these questions anew with him when we meet on common soil, and try to allay his old fears that he would never survive the climate and would ultimately expire in tropical America. By this time he will, of course, have received my letters, all of which make passing reference, among other topics, to his continued and wilful absenteeism.

This evening Mr Brown finally returned after six days' absence on our smaller sister-island's soil. He had little to say, for he seemed exhausted and could stomach barely more than a few mouthfuls of his dinner. Clearly his adjudication had proved long and tiresome, but I cared not to enquire after the details. I could not help but reproach him for his going abroad and leaving only the altogether inadequate book-keeper as the single white person in my immediate company. He must already have received some intelligence of the incidents to which I was making reference, for he chose quickly to apologize and confess it to have been an oversight on his part. He promised to make amends next day. With this our conversation faltered, never to recover, and Mr Brown took his weary leave, leaving me to contemplate my main course in isolation. I, in turn, felt guilty for having pressed him so soon upon his return. These past six days have been the most trying and lonely days I have had to endure. I trust Mr Brown will not again abandon me, unchaperoned, to the caprices of plantation life.

Since the fortuitous return of my vitality, I have almost daily grown increasingly curious to learn more about the nature of the island that I inhabit. Our plantation occupies only one small part of this realm, albeit an enchanting and delectable part, but I dearly wish to taste fully each hidden corner of the land. So it was with a light heart and eager anticipation that I accepted Mr Brown's unexpected and generous offer to spend a day touring with him. He further announced that within the fortnight we would dine in Baytown as the guests of some merchants of his acquaintance. I took the liberty of reminding Mr Brown that on my return to England I intended to occupy myself with a little lecturing, and perhaps even a preliminary attempt at some form of publication. He was kind enough to declare that he could foresee no reason why I should not successfully complete such a project, and that he felt sure that observations gleaned on these two days would augment greatly my proposed study.

The morning sky was brushed with high thin clouds which promised a fine day. A most handsomely attired Mr Brown and I journeyed in a carriage drawn by two stout shire-horses, and we gingerly picked our way downhill, scattering dramatically hued bird-life from ground to twig and branch. Our steep and rocky path, whose nature seemed to have grown more treacherous since my earlier ascent, cut a rough-hewn passage through trees whose overhanging boughs formed a most verdant and magnificent arch. This green architecture allowed entrance to a few cheerful patches of sunlight, and afforded myself and Mr Brown the occasional delightful view of the sea through the dense thicket of trunks and foliage. Below us the waves of the ocean rolled in measured cadence onto the beach, and as we encroached closer the musical harmony of rushing water broke upon our ears with ever-swelling amplitude. On reaching the coastal *island road* the vast expanse of the watery world burst upon our sight and lay spread out before us. Mr Brown kindly informed me that this main highway circumnavigated the whole of this small realm, delicately skirting the watery hem of the island.

We travelled slowly, making full use of the sea-breeze, that friend to sufferers from the conquering heat, essaying only the occasional forays up inland paths in order that Arnold might point out some particular tree, or place of historical interest. Once back upon the main highway, we allowed ourselves but one extended interlude, pausing by a low and loosely assembled stone wall which bordered the road with the high design of guarding against accidents. From over this wall, I peered down at the surface of the sea, smooth and mirror-clear, except where the breakers played over a series of long reefs, far out from shore, and threw up their beautiful but treacherous spray in seemingly playful showers. From ledges upon the face of the rocky precipice on whose summit we stood, sea-birds plumed their ragged feathers and watched alertly for their prey. That great king of birds, the pelican, was on the wing, plying the air, then swooping down to the surface to gather provisions into its ample bill. Sadly, Arnold and I could not tarry long in this sultry atmosphere, for the heat soon became unsupportable and I yearned for that soft cooling breeze brought on by movement of our carriage.

Just beyond the village known as *Butler's*, Arnold drew the carriage to a halt beside a broad stream which coursed through the cane-pieces. He did so in order that I might have the opportunity to observe some negroes engaged in washing clothes. The negro men wore hats, but it was too late to protect their complexions, for nature had already painted them a shade too dark. They did no more than stand and watch as their women performed the domestic ritual, pounding clothes against stones, and then rinsing these rags in the turbid water. The appearance of the females was truly disgusting to me, for without a single exception their arms were drawn out of their sleeves and from the waist upwards they were in a state of unashamed nakedness. One woman, her hair matted with filth, and, I imagine, her flesh host to countless forms of infestation, stood in a condition of total nudity in the centre of the stream. Long encrusted with dirt by her labours, she now scrubbed away at the small rolls of grease with her soapless hands. Eventually she stepped clear of her muddy brown bath, and as the water beaded on the shining surface of her newly bright skin she merely lifted her head to the heavens and imbibed the heat of the sun, which would soon dry her ebon hide. Arnold informed me that such habits of cleanliness were uncommon in these people, who prided themselves on their infrequent use of water. However, where it occurred it was to be encouraged.

Towards midday we reached the capital, Baytown, the point where I began my residence in the West Indies. The town was much as I remembered it. I looked on with barely concealed excitement as a wave of people broke into view, busy, yet no less elegant for that, all occupied with their small colonial businesses. I noticed immediately that in this *city* the spirit of ostentation enjoyed full play in dress. Love of fine fashions appeared to be in vogue, and a solitary shop made much of its knowledge of *home* styles. Every quarter a new delivery of such *elegance*, either direct from London, or from Paris by way of Martinique, found its way into the establishment so that the half-dozen ladies of style might feel comfortably accommodated. Such exquisitely fashioned clothing must, in these climes, give cause to considerable discomfort. Arnold and I observed a cluster of men half melting under heavy, richly embroidered coats and waistcoats, and a solitary English belle clad in the thickest taffetas and satins, some embossed with gold and silver brocades. Even the military men, consisting mainly of Infantrymen and Carbineers, were duty-bound to labour in scarlet wool, which seemed a most unnecessary burden on an already over-worked body of men. Having displayed their courage and won their laurels in the field of Mars, they now seemed embattled and near defeat under the assault of the tropical climate.

Baytown itself boasts perhaps 3,000 to 4,000 persons and no more than 1,000 houses. The greater number of the presentable *white* houses are painted in cool shades and boast covered galleries running along either the side or the front where their inhabitants might gather and enjoy sweet conversation, or simply observe the daily goings-on within their little colony. Many of these dwellings are shaded by abundant trees of all descriptions clustered together in small, but well-tended gardens. The shops are designed in three grades; firstly, a species of wooden room about six or eight feet square which allows the plying of various low trades, such as tanning and the like. Secondly, the stores of the retail provision dealers, which are on a larger scale and supplied amply with goods. Finally, the merchants' stores or warehouses, often annexed to workshops or lumberyards. The other buildings of note include: St George's Church and Churchyard, the Government House, the Arsenal, the Court-House, the *Ebeneezer Chapel*, which rightfully belongs to the members of the Methodist Society (where espionage is carried out to weaken the proper bond between master and slave), and the Gaol, where I am led to believe the men are separated from the women, and the debtors from the cruel felons. The only other meeting-places of note are the grog-shops which play host to crowds of *jetty* revellers, bawds of all shades, and the lower kind of white soldier or sailor. They gather together in these dark places, their eyes and teeth gleaming, and greedily quaff their noxious swill, which must, sooner or later, prey upon their constitutions. To those enervated by age or infirmity, drinking grog remains a last consolation, but by far the greater number of these wretches are in a state of tolerable health. Arnold stopped briefly by the lamp-lit entrance to one such satanic den, where my ears were assaulted by fearsome curses, idiotic laughter, discordant song, and all the stumbling incoherence that accompanies the advanced stages of intoxication.

The streets of Baytown are uncommonly broad and straight, and in places two carriages might comfortably pass without danger to either. On the subject of horse and carriage, Mr Brown was eager for me to observe the lamentable equipage which in these parts is allowed to enter the ranks of the socially acceptable. Two sorry horses, one perhaps of fourteen hands and white in colour, the other a rough brown beast resembling a Shetland pony, are often to be observed shackled incongruously together, sometimes as different in temperament as they are in appearance. I was witness to a debate about the virtues of travelling to the east or to the west conducted by two such jades whose mouths were evidently the most obdurate that had ever tugged against bit and bridle. Their violent contention marooned their hapless driver squarely in the street, he being unable to entreat either beast to give way to the other. Some half-hour elapsed before the *traffic* was once more able to *flow*.

A sight to which I found it difficult to reconcile myself was the number of apparently *free* blacks wandering the streets, shoes on their feet, their unstockinged legs shining like twin columns of jet. It seems that some of these blacks are indeed free, having earned their manumission by their master's generosity, by some good deed, or by thrift and self-purchase, but the majority of these African brethren remain slaves to townsmen, and are employed as servants, porters, and artisans. Black carpenters, coopers, blacksmiths and masons abound, and they are hired out by their owners to assist the other townsmen in their labours. Some are allowed freely to seek labour, but bound to pay their masters a specified sum per day or per week, depending upon the individual arrangement, but the dress, manner and gait of these relatively civilized town slaves marks them off as a wholly different breed from their brutish country cousins.

Owing to a slight misfortune to the heel of my right shoe, Mr Brown and I had reason briefly to present ourselves at the hovel of one of these free negro dandies, having learned that these days no white cobbler was keeping shop-hours in the capital. This black, himself unshod, was busily employed in fashioning, from the most unfragrant materials, a pair of high boots, no doubt destined for the legs of some black exquisite.

As he did so he sang a tune in a minor key which Mr Brown identified as negro music, but which to my ear seemed a corrupt version of an old Welsh air, the name of which I could not recollect. On observing us the black rolled up his eyes until only the whites were visible, and then, holding his little flannel cap in one hand, he prostrated himself before us in a gesture of base supplication. Upon this performance I beat a hasty retreat, determined if need be to hobble all day. Most of the sooty tribe have embraced dully a belief in their own degradation and inferiority, and clearly this is the greatest impediment to their making progress, for self-love can never be as towering a sin as wilful self-neglect. This desperate tendency to despise their own race and colour is one of the ugliest consequences of their miserable condition. However, truly I was unsure, in the case of this *sambo*, whether or not he was making sport of us, for I detected about his free person touches of wit which he appeared to be only partly concealing, but to what purpose I could not fathom. Mr Brown declined to comment.

While the ever-present question of negro civility was pressing upon my mind, Arnold suggested that I might wish to witness the proceedings of a slave-court that was currently in session. As I entered, the delightful cool air of the Court-House struck me sweetly about the brow and banished the heat-induced throbbing which was beginning to assault my person. The interior of this Court-House was fitted up in an elaborate style, and boasted a display of blue paint, intended, one presumes, to give it a commanding yet informal appearance, especially in the warm light of day. To mine own eyes the décor merely conveyed a lamentably shoddy impression more reminiscent of gaudy public Reading-Rooms, or the imagined labyrinths of a Gentleman's place of entertainment. The atmosphere of sobriety that one might properly associate with a place of legal judgement appeared to have played no part in the design of this *creole* palace.

The case before us involved a seventeen-year-old girl, of most disgustingly dirty appearance, originating from the plantation below our own. Her name was Punch, a peculiar appellation which I assumed to be a fond name. Arnold seemed to have some understanding of the details of her case. It appears that she attempted to infuse some corrosive sublimate into the *sangaree* of her master, with the intention of dispatching him to another world. The master, having received warning that such treachery might be abroad, pretended to drink the lethal potion and then observed her reaction by the minute as he went unscathed about his daily duties. Eventually Punch broke down screaming, sure that either a miracle had taken place or her master had by stealth become a *jumby*. The trial appeared to be conducted with reasonable propriety and justice. The jury consisted of three respectable local citizens, the bench of a magistrate presided over by a senior member, who appeared a most pompous coxcomb, no doubt standing mighty high in his own estimation.

In this case of Punch the poisoner there was no legal representation on either side, which circumvented the often laborious and time-wasting process of quiz and counter-quiz, and artful cross-examination punctuated by theatrical appeals to the passions. It is to be greatly lamented that the dangerous practice of perjury is commonplace among negroes. Arnold informed me that some have argued that the condition of ignorance to which the negro is deliberately reduced necessarily renders him unable fully to comprehend the serious obligations of an oath, but history apparently proves this claim false. The negro, whether house-slave or field, bond or free, is likely to fabricate a tale wherein every second sentence will contradict what has gone before. This accumulation of falsehoods is always compounded by his declaring a passionate desire to 'kiss the book', and reinforced with wild assertions of the purest innocence. Mercifully, this Punch appeared to have no defence and was summarily condemned to die, in two days time, by hanging. There was no appeal, and sentence was passed without the least emotion on the part of the magistrates, although tears of pity were apparent enough upon the countenances of the sombre mass of black life that filled the public gallery, plainly aggrieved that the word of the worst scoundrel, were he the possessor of a white skin, would be given preference to their own testament. I asked Arnold whether any white person had been condemned to die for a crime such as killing a slave, but he made reply that were a black to be killed by a cruelly disposed master, in law such cases are considered trifles, for there is usually no reason for a man to deplete his stock without good and just cause. I did not think this is a shining example of rational argument to submit to those in whom one is trying to instill the rudiments of our morality, although Mr Rogers would no doubt vigorously contest the wisdom of making any effort to lead our black brethren and sisters out of their moral darkness. A formal system of law whereby any offender, irrespective of colour or quality, is meted out just punishment, seems not to have taken hold on this island.

At the end of this somewhat afflicting trial, Arnold and I decided not to wait until another negro's fate was sealed. We boarded our carriage and proceeded to the north-east, out of the capital, then turned inland and towards the cooler clime of the hills that nestled in the lee of the mountain. Our interior journey took us along a thin, wearisome track that was truly almost concealed by returning nature. At intervals our path was totally overgrown with tall grass, and in other places made dangerous by the deep ruts created by the seasonal journeys of the sugar carts. Such perils demanded the most skilful handling of our carriage. As we made our laborious progress, our eyes were assailed by an unpleasant sight. We happened upon a small cluster of houses, which, although they did not constitute a village, had a communal aspect about them. These rural dwellings were in general of mean construction, although some few were erected in neatly stacked native stone. One vainglorious hovel sported a well-stocked garden of negro produce, such as eddoe, yam, arrowroot, etc., but even this *mansion* stood destitute of paint. I was startled and horrified to observe that the denizens of this hamlet were white people who had evidently declined financially and morally, having witnessed the estates they worked on sold to meet mortgage debts. Many had arrived in these parts as indentured servants, their period of servitude understood to be seven years, at the conclusion of which their master was to reward them with fifty shillings, four hundred pounds of sugar or tobacco, and a certificate of their manumission. Unable to marry a free person without the consent of their master, the fine for such an illicit connection being – absurdly in view of their extreme poverty – one hundred guineas, they existed in a pitiable state of bondage, and were as likely to be subject to a public whipping or imprisonment as the common negro.

Naturally these poor white *creoles* form an entirely different class from those whites who have emigrated in search of financial gain, or whose government or domestic duties have torn them, albeit temporarily, from the bosom of the land of their birth. Although outnumbered by their superiors, there are not a few of these pale-fleshed *niggers* enduring these lamentable conditions. But not all of these poor-whites came to the island as poverty-stricken indentured servants. Some had suffered from ill-fortune or improvidence, and fallen from the comparative wealth of slave ownership and a position of some standing in the white community, to the depths of poverty and depredation. According to Arnold the most destitute among them now rely upon the kindly benevolence of negroes. These black Samaritans feel pity for the white unfortunates and take a mess of stewed produce, with a proportion of garden-stuff from their own grounds made savoury by a little salt meat, to their old *misses* and *massa*. A few hundred yards beyond this wretched compound I was able to witness the truth of Arnold's claim that the negro sometimes displays a wondrous constancy to these old white attachments. We stopped an old leathery woman, her face lined with a thousand wrinkles, who sucked on what must once have been designated a pipe. Time had bent her form and grizzled her woolly hair, yet her black eyes were never still. Upon her head she carried a basket, and protruding beneath her billowing skirt a monstrous pair of elephant legs completed the picture. As though foreseeing our concern, she entered unbidden into conversation with an aphorism: 'What on the head we no feel, but what on a hand hurt da shoulder.' Arnold smiled and then quizzed her about her destination. She pointed to the basket and spoke emphatically, as though anxious to impress upon us her status. 'I'm carry dem provisions to my old misses for she be very kind to me when I be her nigger; my mistress knowed better times, but bad times now misses, bad times – my misses had plenty nigger, and her husband, and fine pick-a-ninnies, but dem bad times come. Den massa die and misses sell nigger, one, two, three – all gone. Now bad times and so we just go now and den and see misses, and gie her some yam, or some plantain, or any little ting just to help her.' With this the dark benefactress smiled and pressed on with her mission of mercy, with the knowledge that starvation always conquers pride, and that even a dish of negro pottage can be a banquet to the impoverished whites

Arnold and I continued our skyward journey in silence, which gave me the opportunity to survey the beauty of the abundant flora all around. The hill was shaded with trees, the master of which was the carnation. On account of its not growing above ten feet high, this tree can be numbered among those aromatic *shrubs* which exhale the most agreeable fragrances. Its dark crimson flowers were observed to be often spotted with white, its leaves a cool and inviting dark green. Among the other species were the passion flowers, which grew in every hedge and twined around every tree. The passion fruit is a speciality of the tropical table, and everywhere I observed both fruit and flower jointly ornamenting the bush.

Presently we arrived at a grassy clearing where Arnold

instructed two negro servants, Glasgow and Bo, who had travelled independently to rendezvous with us here. They unpacked in silence and began to prepare our luncheon. Arnold and I wandered some twenty yards to the west and discovered a picturesque, shaded, though now deserted cottage, which had the great advantage of a magnificent prospect over the ocean. Hawthorn Cottage, explained Arnold, formerly belonged to a French family who in the earlier days of settlement, when it was imperative for those who suffered religious persecution to find some part of the earth where they might feel safe, happened upon this tropical haven. In recent years the cottage has lain abandoned in this perfect wilderness, allowing tall grasses and climbing weeds unchallenged domain. Yet, despite the bat and the lizard, and other less pleasant creatures who have made it their own, Hawthorn Cottage has remained popular as a picnic site, although rarely do such *al fresco* groups intrude upon one another in this well-concealed location. Arnold suggested that while our black pair completed their task we might stroll through its deserted shell. Like the greater number of West Indian houses, the cottage was built with open rafters and unglazed windows, to allow maximum circulation of air and penetration of light. The wooden shutters (some of which hung sadly) would be raised during the day by means of a long stick, and at night the stick would be withdrawn and the shutter attached to the window-ledge by means of a hook to an eye. The earthen floor was much in need of repair, and it was evident that the chimney would probably deny passage to any smoke, although in this climate it was unlikely that fires would often be lit. But this aside, the cottage appeared functional and somewhat inviting. I lingered awhile until we were disturbed by the all-too familiar bray of negro voices.

In order that we might guard against the intrusion of disagreeable flying pests, as was customary, we employed both our blacks to stand over us while we took luncheon, bearing large pendant branches of the coconut. These they took in their broad negro paws, and waved this foliage backwards and forwards creating a pleasing fragrance while at the same time raising a gentle breeze. I ate quickly, and with the happy appetite of one exhausted by adventurous labour. Arnold turned the conversation back beyond the unpleasantness of the poor white negroes, to the nature of the slave-court, and shared with me his views on the punishment of negroes. 'Judicious firmness' might be a summary of his feelings on this issue, but on one point he was adamant. And this was that only he, among the white men of our plantation, should presume to strike a negro with the omnipotent lash, no matter how great the offence. In addition, no abusive language, as distinct from physical punishment, should be used against them. Clearly Arnold took it upon himself to be the sole authority when it came to justice for the negro. He informed me that he had already discharged one book-keeper on this account, for in a dispute with an African named Israel, the book-keeper had not only kicked the unfortunate negro but had the insolence to assault him with the name, 'dirty nigger'. Apparently the black, Israel, came the next day to see Arnold and made an earnest petition. Four eye-witnesses were summoned, examined separately, and the truth of Israel's ill usage proved. The villifier of the negro remained steadfast in his denial of the assault, but he was discharged after being told that his possession of a white skin was no ground for belief in his word over the negro's. According to Arnold the negroes celebrated this decision for several days.

Unfortunately, sooner than either of us could have possibly imagined, an opportunity presented itself for the testing of Arnold's theories on negro punishment. We returned to the plantation in the late afternoon, travelling the greater part of our upward journey beneath the dense roof of branches which allowed the penetration of only the occasional dim shaft of sunlight. These rare beams splashed on the thin, dusty track, forming small circular pools of light whose shimmer provided the illumination by which we picked our slow way home. No sooner had we stepped from the carriage than we were greeted by a young overseer who was anxious to explain how he had caught the huge negro, Cambridge, purloining meat. Some words had been exchanged during which our man accused of theft apparently insulted the overseer. Hearing this account a tight-lipped Arnold departed in search of the black criminal, and returned some minutes later in a rage and claiming loudly for all to hear that he had been the victim of unprovoked aggression. Arnold decided to act immediately and enquired as to whether I wished to observe *his* court in session. I said I did, and together we retired to the level beneath the piazza where the accused Cambridge and the offended overseer soon presented themselves.

The two issues at stake were, firstly, whether or not Cambridge had stolen the meat and, secondly, whether he had insulted the overseer. That he had committed a further heinous crime of laying hands upon Arnold was beyond doubt, evidenced by my companion's enraged condition. To the second charge the grey-haired black offered no defence. To the first he claimed that he was not stealing, for come Sunday he intended to replace the meat with stock from his own provisions. Arnold asked why permission was not sought to remove the meat if, as he claimed, it would presently be replaced. Cambridge answered, in his polite English, that should permission be sought for every insignificant act then there would be precious little time for work on the plantation. Arnold replied that not everyone was as honest as Cambridge claimed to be, and that only if they were so would such a system be workable. Cambridge then adopted the manner and speech of one familiar with the conventions of the bar and claimed the status of *trustee*, indicating that it was a much lesser position than that of Head Driver, an office which I was astonished to hear him claim he had twice refused. At this point our junior overseer laughed out loud, remarking that the black's insubordinate nature made him ill-suited to the office of *trustee*, but not wishing to be seen to be in opposition to his superior, Mr Brown, he essayed no opinion on Cambridge's capacity to perform the élite role of Head Driver. With time passing, and the argument in danger of becoming circular in form, Arnold decreed that he would suspend judgement. He was concerned that he should not be accused of acting in the heat of the moment, and imposing a wrong verdict in so delicately balanced a case. I have to confess that his decision bore strong witness to the efficacy of my influence, for I feared an instant ruling might ruin the pleasantness of the day we had just spent together. I therefore concurred enthusiastically with his decision, and a conclusion, although not altogether satisfactory, and certainly temporary, was achieved.

At this intermission everybody, the presence of Arnold and myself notwithstanding, retired to their respective quarters. I have still not accustomed myself to the alarming speed with which the tropical day gives way to night, ignoring the lingering deepening of the blue to which those of England are familiar. I stood by the window to my bed-chamber and watched the last embers of daylight die out in dusky red streaks along the horizon, and marvelled as the red ball of the sun buried herself in the heart of the ocean. After the great heat of the day the delightful occasion was to be enjoyed. The possession of an expansive view of the ocean adds greatly to the attractions of the scene, but this theatre seems never truly complete until I descry the image of the mist-bedimmed moon atop the watery world. Only then am I ready to drag my weary bones into my cot, and for many an hour surrender to the feverish caprices of an ill-ventilated dreamworld. And to dream of what? England, of course. And a life sacrificed to the prejudices which despise my sex. Of loneliness. Of romance and adventure. Of freedom.

Some ten days later, as promised, Arnold escorted me back into Baytown where I attended a dinner given at a prominent

merchant's house. I had been led to understand that the dull
expense of formal dinner was being replaced by the latest vogue
of the small social community, where ladies might debate freely
with gentlemen, and thus conversation might replace cardplay
as the main communal resource of a lady's evening. However, I
was to be afforded the opportunity of witnessing the traditional
West Indian dinner, where the table laboured under a burden
of ostentatious and substantial dishes. Gentlemen predominated
numerically. Many brought with them their servants, some in
livery, some not so, some with shoes, some barefoot, but all
truly exemplified the type of the unprepossessing negro. They
buzzed and swarmed around us like flies, and the lack of any
formal arrangement among them created a vast disorder –
excepting, of course, the arrangement whereby they might
attempt to steal from beneath our very gaze whatever might
be carried off.

I believe our merchant host originated in Portugal, but his
table gave no hint of his foreign tastes, laden as it was with
familiar local provisions, which not only now sat easily upon
my stomach but gave so much pleasure to the palate that I began
to wonder if I should ever again adjust to the fare of England.
Was I doomed to become an exotic for the rest of my days? This,
it now seemed to me, would be no bad thing, for I discovered
much at this dinner that warmed my heart towards one class
of these *creole* people. I had heard those engaged in West Indian
cultivation spoken of as choleric and unstable, inclined to be
imperious, but lacking in polish, who having raised themselves
from mediocrity to some form of affluence, now reclined
in tropical ease framing excessively elevated notions of their
birth. However, these plantation managers are hard-working,
up before sunrise, first into the field, and often the last to
leave at night. Since their labour is not purely for their own
benefit, their application is all the more admirable. Men such
as Father, who profit greatly by these managers' labour, would
surely expire were they required to perform a fraction of the

physical and mental tasks that these fellows undertake daily.
At this dinner were two or three planting men who seldom
come to Baytown seeking pleasure, for they are usually too
busy with their agricultural concerns. Baytown is occupied
by, or, rather, abandoned to, those who hold situations under
Government, or attorneys, medical men, merchants, and of
course the military (including naval officers of such ships as
chance to be on station).

Another myth was soon dispensed with, that of drink. Many
a long cork of the rosy *Vin de Bordeaux* was carefully drawn
and the wine poured into the waiting crystal, and bottles
of champagne were unwired, uncorked, and their sparkling
contents offered to all. But although the tongue never remained
idle, fine wit was displayed. The news was eagerly discussed,
and *bons mots* flew like arrows, but no hectic face glowed
excessively, nor were the laughing eyes dampened with anything
other than the dew of happy excitement. It appears that drinking
to excess is seldom practised, although the lower orders, the
book-keepers and white labourers, regularly fall victim to this
vice. I have mixed in society where courtly manners prevail,
and where much art is practised to bestow a polished grace, but
seldom have more sterling qualities of the mind and native good
breeding been displayed than amongst these planters, whose
propriety was such that not for one moment did I suspect any
of aping their betters.

After the dinner, the ladies were not encouraged to remain
long at the table. We retired to the drawing room, where
something like conversation took place. Only the most successful among the managers are able to afford a wife. Her
duties are most arduous. Distant from markets and the few
small civilized comforts that a West Indian town affords, she
must survive upon the stock produced from the estate. With
careful management this can be comfortably arranged. She
must, however, discipline herself to listen to all the stories of
the people on the estate, young and old, and the negro children

must be closely watched. It is her duty to reward the good and admonish the wicked. Those ladies with small children of their own have still more to do, yet in their personal attention towards their offspring they prove the most responsible and affectionate of parents, different in conduct from the fashionable mothers of England who quickly abandon their progeny to the care of negligent mercenary nurses, thereby depriving the leading youth of England of that natural maternal contact which brings forth the balanced mind. As to the practice of education, there is little to be done but to send the older children to Europe, for a newly arrived governess will soon marry. Either this or risk the children falling into a slothful state of ignorance. In later years the boys seldom return, and should the girls do so it is generally to enjoy the chivalry of local eligible bachelors, all intent upon marriage to any passing creature with a fair skin.

In a little time the gentlemen entered, and befogged the room with tobacco smoke. Soon after, a pair of grinning, facetious negroes busied themselves handing around coffee and cake. Sad to recount, those just beneath the status of plantation manager, the overseers, book-keepers and the like, no matter how large the plantations they labour on, generally have not the means to enable them to make any woman decently comfortable. Salaries as small as £200 per annum are not unusual, with of course provision made for what rum, sugar and salt-fish they require from the estate. These overseers and book-keepers are seldom invited to share a merchant's table, but Arnold's situation is a little happier, since following the departure of Mr Wilson, he has assumed the role of manager. His salary and status were now certainly sufficient to warrant his presence, although I felt strongly that he barely tolerated the excesses of our merchant host in order to assist me in my investigation of the white people and their ways. Indeed, as comfortable and welcome as I was made to feel, I could not help but wonder at the pretentious parade of our city company.

Among the merchants, as distinct from the planters, it is

incumbent upon each new host to outdo his predecessor. Furthermore, at the earliest opportunity, newly acquired diamonds and strings of pearls must always be prominently displayed. I was made to understand that it is on the annual occasion of the Governor's Ball that the grand scale of this vulgar extravagance finds its full expression. Female hearts, young and old, beat at the prospect of this eventful night, and the solitary shop which deals in European fashions is crowded with visitors, or their *femmes de chambre*, demanding lace, tiffany and other materials to occupy the busy fingers of a dozen seamstresses. Plying their needles with breathtaking speed, these *tailoresses* are called upon to invent ever-increasingly flamboyant flounces, pinkings and furbelows. This addiction to ornament, at the expense of convenience, is at present a strong characteristic of the West Indies, luxuries abounding where decencies are often found to be lacking. It appears that this is the common consequence of a young civilization lacking the constraints of a polite tradition.

I shared some of Arnold's relief as we entered our carriage and prepared for the journey back towards the comparative sanity of our plantation. The convivial season of Christmas lay some weeks hence, but the spirit of goodwill was already in the air. Before we could take our leave large numbers of over-excited negroes gathered about, begging us to give them some *remembrancer* of the season. This we declined to do, though we did bestow upon each one of them a broad smile. Soon they would receive more tangible rewards, for Arnold informed me that every Christmas the negro enjoys four pounds of pork and two quarters of sugar, with children under twelve receiving half allowance. Often an ox is killed and a fresh portion of meat distributed, and for all the *sambos* this is a time of great merriment during which they regularly powder each other with flour and play contentedly. Even our negro attendants grinned and joked as we made our way back through the pitch black night, but I did, however, suspect some application of the rum encouraged their joviality.

We had travelled for some minutes beyond Baytown before I realized that we were not making directly for our plantation. I glanced at Arnold who chose not to return my concerned enquiry. This being the case, I decided to submit to the capricious nature of this new adventure. To my right the exotic fraternity of a line of coconut trees determined where land ended and sea began. To my left the light breeze combed through the cane-fields producing a coarse, though not unpleasant, whisper. The moon was bright, though not full, and after turning into a narrow ascending lane, I soon recognized the dark silhouette of Hawthorn Cottage looming ahead. Our negro attendants drew the carriage to a halt, and Arnold provided a supportive arm as I stepped down to the ground. Then, to my surprise, but to my relief also, the servile brace retired into the wilderness of tall grasses and left myself and Arnold quite alone. Arnold's first gesture was to turn and look upon me, which he did politely, but I could read about his manner a desire to touch my face. We stood together, neither one daring to breach the silence, until Arnold cleared his throat as though to speak. But he chose to remain silent. He found the courage, I am happy to say, to make contact, and very soon we felt able to hold each other. Perhaps the heat has introduced some weakness of character into my person, but I must confess to not feeling any guilt as a result of this new intimacy. If the truth be told, the single emotion that came rushing into my body was that of happiness; pure, undistilled, happiness at my good fortune to have discovered a man such as Arnold in the tropical backwater of the Americas.

It often happens in life (and certainly in the novels with which I used to amuse myself in England), that at precisely the moment one expects fortune to smile, clouds of doom descend and obscure that sweet countenance. Not a fortnight has passed by since the merchant's dinner, yet the atmosphere about the plantation has suddenly deteriorated from the levity that

one associates with the preparations for Christmas, to sinister
intrigue and fear. The goddess *Discord* has flourished her arms
and ushered in *wordy war*, causing the whole neighbourhood to
rise in commotion. The question is the recurrent one of what to
do with the recalcitrant African, Cambridge. I have been unable
to discover his full history from Stella, for she is reluctant to
speak of him, save to inform me in her grotesque lingo that
he is a good man and in the right in these continual skirmishes.
'Missy, he good man. You no know what dat man suffer.'
Stella did, however, confirm that in spite of all the barriers
in his way, this Cambridge is lettered, can read his Bible, and
even endeavours to teach it to his fellow blacks, which leads me
to conclude that, indeed, this *ancient* Cambridge is no ordinary
negro. Furthermore, it appears to be the case that Mr Brown
did in fact offer Cambridge the position of Head Driver as part
of his plan to compel some lesser drivers to accept relegation
to lowly positions, such as watchmen, and thereby undermine
long-established bonds of friendship and loyalty between the
field-slaves. Unfortunately, Cambridge refused to collaborate
with Mr Brown's scheme. And now this festering conflict has
caused some friction between myself and my companion, Stella,
though this difficulty merely mirrors the larger conflict between
black and white on the plantation.

Dancing, music, and jesting, after the negro fashion, seem to
have ceased. They have been replaced with men who, eyes half
closed, loll against a wall, or lie inert upon a sunny bank, and
wilfully doze away leisure hours until called upon to return with
reluctance to the labours of the field. Beyond the staring whites
of their eyes, and the glittering rows of dazzling teeth, I can now
see that the saturnine house-servants look upon me with a new
suspicion. As soon as they think me out of earshot they renew
their animal chatter as though I am in some way responsible for
this disagreeable situation. They obviously assume that I am
prejudiced on the side of the young overseer in this irksome
dispute, but in this they are mistaken. I am merely waiting for

Arnold to dispense his justice, being confident that whatever decision he reaches will most likely be the correct one.

A second cause for concern is Christiania, who has chosen this moment to disappear. Again the plantation is divided along rather crude lines, with the blacks having some knowledge (or so we feel) of her whereabouts, and the whites wishing to have her declared a runaway and so set in motion a hunt for her black hide. Should she be recaptured she will naturally be thoroughly flogged or else transported, a punishment which the majority of the whites, having been compelled to endure the arrogance of this woman, would dearly wish to see. It would be difficult for the outsider properly to discern the nature of this unhappy atmosphere, for it is possible that the stranger might mistake this sourness of heart for the feelings that normally occur in this clime, and indeed fail to recognize anything particular amiss. But to those of us, black and white, who are familiar with plantation life, this new unease is causing deep distress.

This morning, over breakfast, I chanced to mention to Arnold that he might consider arriving at his decision before Christmas. He asked me which decision, clearly now conscious of the double judgement in his keep. I took it upon myself to suggest that the decision over Cambridge was the more urgent of the two, for the curious behaviour of this over-confident, Bible-reading slave demanded immediate attention. I confessed to Arnold that to my observation this bondsman had about his gaze an unsound quality. Furthermore, I insisted that he seemed determined to adopt a *lunatic* precision in his dealings with our English words, as though the black imagined himself to be a part of our white race. Arnold mused on all that I said, then added that because the blacks were destroying the goodwill of the Christmas season he would soon pronounce upon Cambridge. If necessary, the matter of Christiania could wait until the new year for it seldom happened that a runaway managed to leave the island. In the case of this witless negress, successful flight to a distant shore seemed highly unlikely. We ate in silence for a short while, until I asked Arnold if surely there was not something else that was troubling him. I insisted that the circumstances of my being on the island could not, of course, be permitted to unseat the established system of discipline which secures the labour and obedience of the slaves. Arnold said nothing. I continued, pointing out that although I suspected a woman such as myself must occasionally prove an intolerable nuisance for one such as Arnold, I was prepared to risk tarnishing my own reputation as good company if only I might provide him with a secure vessel into which to pour his well-corked grief.

Eventually Arnold spoke, but he would not look me in the eye, offering only the cropped pate of his head. He admitted that due to a virulent strain of cane-blight the sugar was not as healthy as he had hoped, and he feared for the financial returns on this year's harvest. This worry was compounded by the fact that an overseer close to Arnold (although he was too discreet to divulge the man's name) had developed the powerful dispatcher known as the yaws, a terrible and obstinate contagion transmitted by illicit coupling with a black. On making its nauseous appearance the yaws brings with it frightful ravages, twitching pains extending to the very marrow, and a loathsome deformity of bone and flesh. The disease leaves the afflicted wretch at a distance from his fellow kind, often abandoned by man and left to the mortal office of nature. Recovery, although rare in older sufferers, demands cleanliness, a nutritious diet without meat or salt animal food, and the dedication to observe this strict regimen despite the inward signs of pain and the outward signs of humiliation. Poor Arnold! That he should be compelled to observe such sufferings! This season of goodwill was rapidly becoming a nightmare for him. He took himself up to return to work with the spirit and posture of a man only too aware of approaching mortality.

How 'flat, stale and unprofitable' life can sometimes be! I speak now of Mr McDonald, who has just interrupted my afternoon rest to pay me an unsolicited visit. What is more,

I fear his true purpose is out, for he asked me, in the manner of a hurt schoolboy, if it were true that I had dined with Mr Brown at a merchant's home. I answered in the affirmative, and added that I had enjoyed a pleasant evening, particularly the company of Arnold. Mr McDonald seemed somewhat taken aback by my confirmation of this and pleaded that he had any number of invitations to dine at all the influential houses on the island, and that he would be pleased if I might one day consider accompanying him. Without wishing to cause offence to Mr McDonald, I made it quite clear I already had a companion with whom I was more than satisfied. I indicated that it might make life difficult for all parties were I to be seen abroad with another man, and then I passed the situation back into his own no doubt capable hands and directly asked did he not think that this might be the case? Mr McDonald fell speechless. Jealousy is not an uncommon expression of the female temperament, but I believe its appearance in the male is altogether less openly displayed. Mr McDonald sat for some time staring at the space above my head, struggling with his emotions, not knowing my person well enough to declare, yet hoping that upon a hint I might speak. Upon the second, third, and perhaps even fourth hint, I had still not spoken. This was truly a painful encounter, and for the first time I realized what it can cost a man to declare his affection when he doubts a response. In a burst of generosity I attempted to free Mr McDonald from his dilemma by divulging I had information that a ship had been announced, and that I would probably leave for England soon after the Christmas festivities. This served its purposes, for Mr McDonald realized that he would now be excused on more equitable ground. He made a gesture or two in the direction of trying to persuade me to stay on for a few months longer, but then he took his departure. I watched as his carriage began to pick its way down the hill, and then I sighed as it disappeared into a parcel of breadfruit trees. Men, like polite women, should learn to restrain and control their emotions. I retired to my chamber and looked into my mirror. Perhaps the affections of all these men turn in due course to some brown-faced beauty.

This day has marked the beginning of the end of my sojourn in tropical America. Christmas is almost upon us and we should, black and white alike, be enjoying a period of rejoicing and spiritual renewal. Instead, I am daily subjected to tensions which test my fragile nerves, so much so that almost by the hour I feel myself sinking back into that weak state which so marred my arrival on this island. Mr Wilson has reappeared. I can find no other way to describe his appeal to my person, other than that he has thrown himself upon my mercy. I was relaxing after breakfast when Stella ushered onto the piazza a somewhat agitated black boy, who delivered a message in the incoherent slobber of negro speech that I should attend Mr Wilson in a Baytown boarding house. A hastily scribbled note, in what I assumed to be the hand of Mr Wilson, informed me that he had heard from a visitor to the neighbouring island, to which he had been exiled, that I had attended the merchant's dinner. According to his *spy*, I appeared to be a tolerant and well-mannered lady. I bade the excitable negro youth sit, and could not help but observe the affection that these poor blacks seemed to have for Mr Wilson. Stella beamed brightly, for truly a favourite had returned. After a moment's reflection I ordered my skittish sable duenna to have a carriage and pair prepared, for I determined that if I was going to rendezvous with this Mr Wilson I would do so before the sun was high.

En route, one slight unpleasant incident served further to try my fragile constitution. A few hundred yards beyond the village of *Middle Way*, I was accosted by a two-parts naked, one-part tattered little she-slave walking rapidly and energetically along the road. Upon her skull she sported a thick black mat of frizzy wool, and through the thick encrustation of dirt I was able to discern the blackest, most leathery skin. Her sole request, with proffered claw, was the irresistibly ludicrous, 'Misses, misses, you please to buy me a comb for me to tick in me head.' The unfragrance of the negro came from earth, not heaven, and I was obliged to clap a lace handkerchief to my mouth and nose as we took our leave of this mahogany imp. A mile to the north-west of Baytown I espied some sassafras trees putting forth deliciously fragrant tassels of leaves and blossoms which enabled me to remove my handkerchief. These flowering shrubs, along with others new to my acquaintance, enchanted me with their strangeness, as did the wonderful butterflies which seemed to me almost as large as birds.

The rooming-house to which Mr Wilson's negro escorted me appeared to be in a most ruinous and battered condition. It was surrounded by a tiny strip of garden-ground that was barely rescued from the stretch of sandy deposit which bore the weighty name of *street*. From the vantage point of my carriage I might descry that the exterior paint of this dwelling had long since peeled away, that damaged boards needed repairing and in some parts replacing, and I imagined that there could not be a hinge upon any door that had not been long in the deepest need of oil. Instructing my negro driver not to stray, I followed Mr Wilson's black messenger into the dark interior and on into a small room where my father's former manager, a robustly built, though now ageing man, sat with his onerous new companion, poverty. The whole furniture of his room consisted of a chair, a wooden bench, a basin, a ewer, and a relic of soap of great antiquity. I saw a stained towel, and a glass for one's teeth, but little else. The open window of the room commanded an uninterrupted prospect of the *kitchen*, an open shed unfit for the stabling of a horse. There being evidently neither hostess nor chambermaid to serve me, Mr Wilson himself presented me with a glass of *sangaree*. Then, without more formalities, he rapidly engaged me in conversation, explaining that he had been banished by Mr Brown at gunpoint. Mr Brown, he declared, will brook no discussion on any topic; although Mr Brown is a good *cane-man*, fear, not debate, is his method of government. In short, he seemed keen to impress upon me that through a perverse stubbornness Mr Brown was mis-managing and abusing the property of my family, and that had Mr Wilson not been in fear of his life he would never have abandoned the estate. Mr Wilson's parting shots on the subject of Mr Brown were to assure me that, by nature, overseers are inclined to be irascible, but this man's nerves ceased to be under control once the sun was vertical!

Briefly our conversation floundered, then I explained to Mr Wilson that although I knew relatively little of island life I had been reliably informed that he had been dismissed for theft. At this Mr Wilson threw back his head and roared with laughter. Stealing! Did I not know that he was the most steadfast of Christians? In his whole life he had never stolen so much as a fruit from a bush. His only crime, he told me, was over-zealous civic pride, and a care for the welfare of the slaves. He had pursued the maximum profit compatible with humane decency. He was, he insisted, unwilling to see the negroes suffer the debilities brought on by cruel oppression for the sake of naked profit. His laughter took on something of the quality of bitter rage, so fiercely did he continue to mock the suggestion that he could be guilty of theft. By now I was so confused that my feverish head had begun to spin anew. I listened perplexedly as Mr Wilson lectured me on civic pride, claiming that despite the providence of God and nature, there was little that could be called beautiful in the West Indian townships, for nobody cared. The streets were poorly laid out, the public and private buildings mostly clumsy wooden structures, and only the churches and Government House had a scrap of style or dignity. True enough, inside of these ramshackle buildings things could be quite tidy, and even comfortable at times, but neither outward appearance nor civic amenity seemed to be given any consideration.

Mr Wilson, seemingly oblivious of my manifest distress, pressed on, condemning the unpaved streets, the great abundance of verminous rats, insects and reptiles which soiled both street and dwelling place. I wondered about the neighbouring island on which Mr Wilson had sojourned, and asked after him if it were any better cared for. On this topic he dilated at length, claiming that neither it, nor any of these English islands, could boast anything worthy of a glance. They were the holding stations for those who simply wished to extract profit to be lavished on English gaming tables and other more domestic vices. Mr Wilson seemed happy to admit that his unpopularity with the white citizens stemmed from his inclination to speak candidly upon such matters. According to Mr Wilson, what led to his downfall was his defence of a free black from the abuse of power by a petty white retailer. While Mr Wilson was occupied with this philanthropy, Mr Brown, with the assistance of the lesser orders of white power, conspired to unseat Mr Wilson, though he gained much public support from the blacks and even the responsible whites when the black was magically acquitted and the retailer fined. Much to the dismay of the blacks, Mr Wilson was then compelled to run for his life from the mob of whites.

This really was too much. I protested, pointing out that in the not too-distant past Mr Brown had been involved in litigation which resulted in the punishment of a book-keeper for alleged abuses of a slave. My host smiled and commented that perhaps the petty tyrant Brown is learning that it is not possible forever to conceal injustice. I cautiously concurred, then quickly added that it was not possible for me to know for I did not have access to the mind of Mr Brown. Following a rather uneasy silence, I rose to my feet and proposed that it might be better for all concerned if I took my leave. Mr Wilson had the good grace to acknowledge that he was aware that I lacked the power of either censure or discipline, and with this he escorted me to the street. Mr Wilson told me that he would lodge at this rooming-house until the new year, when he planned to return to England, as fortune would have it, by the same ship on which I was due to travel. We bade each other an uneasy farewell, for I was unable to disguise the distress that our discussion had laid upon me. Upon my return I retired swiftly to my bed-chamber, where

I called Stella to attend to me. I asked for some thin gruel to drive out the cold for the strength was rapidly quitting my weak womanly body.

This fierce headache has reduced me to a parlous state. No words can describe my sense of the foulness of the fervid climate that grips and chokes me. My miserable sweltering days are no different from one another than are the sands on the shore. I understand that Arnold has asked for my company, but I instructed Stella to inform him that my lamentable condition would admit of no visitors. There has been no further communication. I feel a gulf is forming between myself and Arnold. He must surely be aware of my audience with his adversary. And what of Arnold's decision regarding the slave Cambridge? Has he finally come to some independent judgement? Poor Mr Wilson, who has suffered so much in his struggle to maintain his values and his dignity. And, of course, poor me. Mr McDonald has paid me a brief and disturbing visit. Surely Arnold will not consider abandoning me now. The revelry has begun anew. The negroes seem to have put aside their troubles and intend to celebrate this imminent Christmas with their customary wild romp, there being little to choose in such cases between savages and children. And what of Father, no doubt deep in his cups at the Planters' Club in London, or swilling champagne in some other company of gentlemen? I can only assume that a *romantic* liaison with some vulgar cockneyess will provide him with his Christmas supper. Does he have no conception of what would claim us all in the tropics were we to slip an inch below the surface of respectability? In these climes all is possible. Perhaps this is why a certain type of man (and woman) longs to settle in these parts. I do not know. How can I know? I have so much still to learn.

How maddening are the senses, how deafening is the heart as life creeps upon her determined course with scant regard for the injuries that are daily afflicted upon mankind, let alone my poor soul. In the midst of all the tumult of this supposed festivity, a threnody of distress is borne upon the gale. Christmas day and Mr Brown dead. Ambushed returning from church by the same *intelligent* negro with whom he waged a constant war. I must bear some responsibility, for it was I who first encouraged Arnold to delay his decision so that I might enjoy a selfish evening, free from the emotional stresses that a stern and decisive judgement would have placed upon it. And now the negro is hanged from a tree, no longer able to explain or defend his treacherous act. The white people of this island dispatched him as a summary warning to any other negroes who might consider such a mutinous path. I cannot relate the full details of the event, but the haughty black woman Christiania had made her return and was in some way involved. It would not surprise me to discover that others of the blacks have been caught up in this motiveless savagery.

Stella brought Mr McDonald to visit with me again. I lay restlessly upon my bed consumed with a fierce and malignant fever. The Scotchman examined me and retired. Like all white people of the region, he now works with a threatening dark cloud above his head. He returned and informed me that he would sit with me on the next day, and that I may need a sick-nurse. His shame was such that he was unable to meet my eyes. His shame! It is clear that I am in no condition to contemplate a long sea-passage. At the same time I have no wish to remain upon this plantation. In my mind I know the place to which Stella and I will retire until I regain my vitality. My present dereliction leaves me without peace.

Mr Wilson has resumed authority to a clamorous welcome, but he has now the unpleasant task of guiding the heathen slaves towards gathering the very poorest of crops. I am led to understand that my father has been sent for, as there is concern not only for my health, but for the condition of the estate. It would appear that a major scandal may yet break and shatter the reputations of divers persons. O lucky Isabella that she never lived to see these shores, never lived to witness the treachery of the negro that some would set free to wreak havoc upon our persons. Their lying subservience, their sly pilfering, their murderous violence, mark them out as very like the Irish, but of an even more childish character. If this overworked land possesses a soul it has indeed been profoundly abused and made to endure much that is evil. Poor Emily. Lucky Isabella, who would always tell me, with regard to my native England, that I must never allow myself to grow old in a country that is unkind to me. Lucky Isabella that she did not live to witness the consequences of her urgings. Stella is but a sad black imitation. Lucky, wise, Isabella.

II

Pardon the liberty I take in unburdening myself with these hasty lines, but thanks be to God for granting me powers of self-expression in the English language. I humbly beg that those of my dear England, Africans of my own complexion, and *creoles* of both aspects, might bear with me as I attempt to release from within my person the nature of my extraordinary circumstances. Soon, I know not when, I am to be dispatched. To where, I know not.

Of my early life in the bosom of my family I confess to having little knowledge. On this subject my memory is no more. In my mind I hold a faded portrait of father and mother and brothers and sisters, but their names and occupations have long-since deserted me. That they loved me is not in doubt. In our unsullied state we are a simple and unwarlike people. It is only the cursed avidity for wealth, and the consequent cruelty, knavery, and practice of diabolical arts by English navigators that has turned the hearts of my simple people from natural goodness, and honest affection, towards acts of abomination. Many natives in my home country are canting, deceitful people about whom one must exercise great caution. The treachery of some of our petty kings, encouraged as they are by so-called Christian customers, leaves one in no doubt that gratitude, that most desecrated of words, has long since fled their crude language. In their dealings my people are great traders and bargainers, having much in common with the Hebrew people in these and other respects. But one should be ever alert and remember from whom my people imbibed the new chicanery. These *Christian* inheritors of the Hebrew tradition have corrupted the virtues of former times.

No longer was I to tarry in my Africa, where my father and mother loved me with a sincere warmth. A storm broke about our dark heads and I, who can remember only my true Guinea name, Olumide, from amongst the many words of youth, was washed towards the coast and away from my rich and fertile soil by *Christian* Providence, whose unlikely agents were those who drink deep of strong liquors, which serve only to inflame their national madness, the slave trade. The Lord intended commerce to enable man to develop the friendly bent of his social affections. Finding his brothers in scattered locales it was hoped that man might forge the sweet blessed security of peace and friendship, while diffusing the goods and commodities of his native land. Such enterprise, with Christian religion as its true companion, would be of profound benefit to any shore fortunate enough to be rewarded with the arrival of traders with soldier-like fortitude, and honest values. It sours my blood that in the Guinea of my youth it was not to be the good fortune of my brethren to meet such men, for unfortunately our shores were visited by those whose eyes were blinded, and hearts stupefied, by the prospect of profit. These men violated the principles of sound commercial policy, and imposed upon their own nation a heavy burden, both moral and financial, for the maintenance of their addiction to slavery. Worse still, they involved the good people of their country in the sorrowful guilt of upholding such a system, thus fusing prejudice into their souls and hardening their hearts.

When I imagine myself to have been not yet fifteen years of age, I was apprehended by a band of brigands and bound by means of a chain to hand and foot. I must confess, to the shame of my fellow Guinea-men, that I was undoubtedly betrayed by those of my own hue. But it remains true that without instruction and encouragement my native people might never have hardened their hearts and tainted the generous customs of their simple country. Shackled unceremoniously to a fellow unfortunate at both stern and bow, we unhappy *blacks* formed a most miserable traffic, stumbling with jangling resignation towards our doom. About my neck I sported a decoration of gold placed there by my mother's own *fair* hand, and from my ears hung larger and less delicate gold pieces of shape, though mercifully not size, resembling the orange fruit. These paragons of virtue who had possession of my body, if not my soul, soon divested me of these trappings, thus breaking off my tenderly formed links with my parents. In addition to this loss, I was forced to endure pain the like of which I had never suffered.

Come night, our dark and snake-ish company fell into the undergrowth and descended into sleep peopled by demons of the imagination. In the morning I vigorously rubbed these visions from my eyes. Native conversation was forbidden and punishable by the lash. Day and night our ears were forced to admit their English talk which, at this stage, resembled nothing more civilized than the manic chatter of baboons. Sleep often endeavoured to elude my malnourished carcass, and on such occasions I would observe these long-haired spirits crouching feverishly around their bright fire, but I knew not whether they craved heat or if they simply feared animals. Their desire to populate the night with a brackish sacrifice formed a regular part of our uninspiring itinerary. I wondered constantly if these men of no colour, with their loose hair and decayed teeth, were not truly intent upon cooking and eating us, for they seemed overly fond of flesh, carrying about them pounds of salted meat for sustenance. Should they exhaust their supplies and feel desire rise within them for fresh quantities, it seemed to me only natural that they should turn to these helpless specimens in their charge. That Christian instruction forbade such *Araby* I was not to discover until some years later when I had the good fortune to fall under the spell of Miss Spencer of Blackheath, who, acting according to the renowned charity of her heart, sought to instill in my dull person the rudiments of Sabbath worship and all that proceeds thereof. However, while dressed in the spiritual and physical guise of *Mungo*, I truly feared the ignominy of being torn limb from limb and devoured as some worthless trifle. Lacking a family or friends with whom I might share the powerful terror of my heart, and being forbidden upon pain of death to forge verbal links with my fellow-sufferers, I would often console myself by pouring out my complaints to the very trees and bushes which masked the paths and trails along which we laboured. To them alone I recounted my sorrows, for I viewed these outer garments of nature as my only companions in life. I lamented what I took to be my own wicked heart which rendered me helpless and in this undone state, and in consequence I suffered great misery knowing not the name of God and being therefore unable to pray for His blessing and bestow thanks upon His holy name. Although ignorance prevented my making direct appeal to the author of all my comforts, He must have been sensible of my plight for Almighty God spared me while others were taken up and ushered into the next world in a multiplicity of agonies compounded by extreme sullenness. This feast of suffering was a result of the actions of these vilest of sinners.

On reaching the coast we of the despised complexion were made to understand something of the magnitude of our fall from grace. The sea saluted our reddened and miserable eyes, and pain assaulted our proud African hearts. We acknowledged by means of mutual looks of fear, the understanding that we had arrived at the edge of the known world. But we were in error. The presence of a large wooden vessel riding at anchor led us to believe that our journey – far from having achieved its natural conclusion – had not even commenced. None among us dared imagine what inhospitable regions lay beyond the waters. Surely the Lord Almighty was with me at this time, and I believe He whispered to me, a poor heathen, words of comfort. So great was His mercy that He took me in hand and enabled me to reign over my quaking terror. We bondaged brethren were herded aboard the vessel with scant consideration for age or infirmity, and treated with less regard than one might bestow upon the basest of animals. We were led to understand by other black fellows, who were evidently in the keep of these white men, that we were not to be devoured. We were informed that soon we would be transported to the white man's country, and once there sold and put to work. These human flesh merchants (for that indeed is what they were) acted towards us with such savagery and brutal cruelty that it remained difficult to believe that they expected profit to be extracted by our eventual sale. We were addressed by one common word, *nigger*, as though we all shared this harsh name. Clearly it was a term lacking in affection, for when it was applied it was commonly partnered by a snarl and a cuff or lash. I was later to learn the truth of this vulgar and illiberal word; it is truly a term of great abuse.

The uncivilized crew made it known that we were to be lodged below deck. One last brief glimpse of the shore was all that we were able to snatch. We fellow captives fixed our watery eyes upon the land in a state of mortal grief. Whether affection for one's country is real or imagined, it is not an exaggeration to proclaim that at this moment instinct of nature suffused our being with an overwhelming love for our land and family, whom we did not expect to see again. Our history was truly broken. With much rough handling and unnecessary ferocity, we were now ushered down into a place of perpetual night. Once below our bodies received a salutation of supreme loathsomeness in the form of a fetor, which affected a manifold increase in the constant grieving and pining which echoed among we brethren. The heat of the climate, the number of cargo, the necessity for loathsome deeds in this common space, soon rendered this wretched situation impossible. It was to be some days before the vessel set forth. In this time many died where they lay, some on top of others, until the whole scene became one of inconceivable horror. The white men came below with eatables. Those who found the strength to refuse were lashed, often to death. It appeared that bitterness and cruelty were sterner masters than mere avarice. Such malice as these men of very indifferent morals exhibited, I had never witnessed among any people. Their most constant practice was to commit violent depredations on the chastity of female slaves, as though these *princesses* were the most abandoned women of their species. These white vulgarians disgraced not only their nation, but the very name of man.

There is much more I could tell of our hateful sea-passage, but to do so, even at this distance of years, still introduces trembling into my person. Many a time, when invited to the deck to take fresh air and flex our bodies, did my countrymen and myself wish to offer up our hopeless lives to the ocean and leap towards the depths. Sadly, we were tightly chained and closely guarded by our keepers. Such was the severity of our captivity that we were denied even the power over our most fundamental and inevitable destiny; that of our demise. There is one act that I can pluck from this traveller's nightmare and cherish as evidence of the heart's power over the villainous mind of others; a fellow Guinea-man, when clearly in the throes of expiration, chose to bestow upon myself his pap to help nourish my ailing body. No words passed between us, and indeed the proffered gift proved distasteful, but I was overwhelmed with gratitude for his human gesture. None but those who have been truly desperate in mind and body can judge of my feelings at this time. Soon after my benefactor escaped his captivity and triumphed. He silently paid the debt of nature and began a new journey into a world beyond the wickedness of the ship. The Almighty Lord will have amply rewarded him with the gift of His everlasting love.

We, the pitiable black cargo, arrived in the Carolinas, North America, after a singularly unpleasant passage during which, bereft of the means to deliver supplicating addresses, we were forever punished under the feet of cruel tyrants. What a feast of benevolent hearts we had been marooned with! It was at this moment of landfall that my soul entered its period of darkest night, for my brethren were ushered from my sight and onto shore. Their fear caused an uproar the like of which I never again desire to endure. Our *guardians* seized a stratagem to appease their grief; that of the whip, plentifully applied. Having witnessed the dispersal of all my companions, I now resigned myself to the fate of being devoured by my captors. I was exceedingly miserable, and, believing myself undone, I desired my life to be extinguished.

My pining was eventually interrupted by one of my own tint, clad in their livery. Using my native tongue he informed me of my new state. I was not to tarry in the Americas (which by false design I had bargained to be the sole abode of white men), for it was intended that I should journey on to England, the original home of the white man, and 'serve *massa*'. With this information transferred my American *countryman* took his speedy leave, but my *massa* neglected to present himself. This not unnaturally caused me great anguish, for I desired to visualize the captain of my fate. Some days later, having jettisoned the human cargo and taken on board fresh provisions, we hauled anchor and set sail for England. I now found myself quartered in new surroundings above the level of the hold. Resembling neither comfort nor hell, but falling somewhere between the two, one might imagine my relief on discovering that I was not expected to undergo a second, and this time solitary, passage below deck. But still I worried. Furnished with only a board upon which to extend my ulcerated limbs, I waited in trepidation for the onset of white hunger, sure that I would be press-ganged into service.

A week of passage eclipsed during which I learned to agree

with English meats and drinks, and during which the Christmas day fell, whereupon I was rewarded with a day's allowance of fresh beef. Washed and clothed now in the English manner, I received verification of the truth of my position by a first sighting of my master, who endeavoured to convince me of his peaceful nature by the laying on of hands and other entreaties. Upon his departure a whiskered clerk in excess of fifty years of age, who to judge by his very *bookish* demeanour was clearly a recipient of much formal education, was appointed to help me smatter a little imperfect English. By degrees I came to understand most communications about me, whether addressed directly or overheard. My clerk, John Williams, a most amicable native of Norfolk, showed me great attention, seemingly without concern for my complexion. He displayed neither shame nor fear at his association with one such as I, and for my part I found it difficult to believe my fortune in finding some person with a mind superior to prejudice. His kind nature helped to dispatch the consternation I suffered because of the ill-bred abuse of the vulgar crew. During the course of this long passage they derived great pleasure by informing me that declining quantities of food meant they would soon have to kill and eat me. Having had the good fortune to fall in with John Williams, my heart quaked only moderately, as he supplied truthful information to drive out their falsehoods.

John Williams instructed me in the gentlemanly art of dressing hair (although with my wool he quickly retired). All the while he made improvement to my English language so that others soon came to comprehend my responses to words addressed. On the dark subject of my name he was unable to assist, and the will of my captain prevailed. No longer Olumide, but Thomas. My captain, a serious man who celebrated the Sabbath by reading prayers to the ship's crew, rewarded me with a flurry of cuffs when I chose to ignore the title Thomas and wait on Olumide. John Williams beseeched me to submit to Thomas, arguing most persuasively that my condition far out-ranked my betrayed brethren, whose backs were breaking under perpetual toil while I carried only the featherish burden of a new name. He asked me if I had not, only the previous day, witnessed a white man flogged unmercifully with a mass of rope and then tossed over the side of the ship as one might spurn a disobedient dog? I was to understand, by virtue of the reasoning of John Williams, that white men's cruelty to white men was often savage. Little would be spared should my idle cuffing find cause to swell into a more powerful signal of displeasure. So, this is how Olumide became Thomas. Some time later every heart was gladdened when sight of merry England was announced. Every heart but my own, for now I was obliged to give up my John Williams, and he I, and we parted with the shedding of tears on both sides.

London, the most enviable capital in the world, was destined to be my home for the greater part of the next decade. My master made it known that I was to consider myself his domestic, not his slave, and he spoke in a manner which suggested abhorrence of the trade which had occasioned his fortunes to increase. I soon came to understand that English law had recently decreed trading in human flesh illegal, so I learned to perceive of my master as a criminal. However, he was but one of a large multitude of contented plunderers happily accommodated in the bosom of English society. My master lodged me in the servants' quarters of his Pall Mall home where a supplementary attendant, a woman of my own clime and complexion, Mahogany Nell, serviced his needs. To my dismay these included his frequently admitting her to his bed. Although her pigmentation might not be as engaging as that of the fair daughters of Albion, my master clearly derived much comfort through his actions, for they were frequent and, if my ears did not deceive me, brutal in their lengthy pleasure. His sole servant beyond the dark pair (of whom I was one) comprised a sturdy Englishwoman by the name of Anna, who appeared to be deemed unworthy of fleshy exploration. We four, my master included, contrived to create a colourful kingdom of peace in this Pall Mall to which we were bound by fate. We domestic servants waited upon my newly retired master (for I was the final piece in his stratagem of pensioned ease), cleaning, cooking, attending to his toilet, determining that he should want for nothing. He was not of that breed of retired captain who delighted in displaying his good fortune in gaudily laced coats and cocked hats. His only marks of distinction were his black servants, but thankfully we were never pressed to shadow him in the streets. My master grew fond of his black Tom, and I loved him in return. I would observe his manner, and by my actions I hoped to introduce him to the notion that my sole pleasure in life derived from the great privilege of being able to serve him. It was he who, as my dexterity with English words multiplied, informed me that I was at liberty to walk about this great city and gather intelligence which might help me further appreciate my situation. I daily found my predicament becoming more agreeable, and I thanked him most profusely in his own words. Mahogany Nell and Anna near-burst with joy on hearing my first true and unaided speech, which contained many phrases strung confidently together.

Armed with an enhanced mastery of this blessed English language, I went forth into London society and soon discovered myself haunted by black men occupying all ranks of life. To my great surprise I found men of colour and ladies of complexion who walked the higher streets and occupied the gardens of the formal and distinguished squares. These *darling* blacks were effectively shielded from the insults of the vulgar, but I was soon to discover that the source of their fortunes often lay in the desire of the Englishman and the Englishwoman to take up a black or brown *companion* as a fashionable appendage. Lower down the ranks were the destitute blacks: harlots, entertainers, assorted vagabonds, a motley congregation of *Jumbo*'s and *Toby*'s, many of whom exhausted what bronze they could beg or pilfer swilling down that most famous national cordial, best gin. The bustling narrow cobbled streets of London were indeed teeming with a variety of unfortunate negroes. Black men too feeble to work were often turned adrift in their decay of health, and the *useless* women were generally reduced to advertising themselves as capable of 'performing the rites of Venus as they are done in the Carib seas'. These sad females elicited much bawdy laughter from young bloods and civilized men alike, the quality of their usage being the object of much coarse speculation. It was the *comical* street entertainers who were the real aristocrats of the destitute blacks, and chief among this ungodly scourge was one who sported a wooden leg and a quite ludicrous hat. I suspect this man is more responsible than most for fixing us in the minds of the English people as little more than undignified objects for their mirth and entertainment.

John Williams introduced me to the Christian religion while I dwelt on board the ship. Unfortunately, I was unable to make a coherent sense of either his words or his ideas, being more concerned with avoiding English jaws and my possible fate as meat to match their drink. But after talking awhile with Anna, and marvelling at her pure and godly thoughts, I begged my master for full and proper instruction in Christian knowledge so that I might be received into Church fellowship with both experience of the Bible and a conviction of belief. To this end my master, at his expense and with his blessing, sent me to study under a Miss Spencer of Blackheath, who proved a most patient and virtuous instructress. I earnestly wished to imbibe the spirit and imitate the manners of Christian men, for already Africa spoke only to me of a barbarity I had fortunately fled. To this end, I embraced this magical opportunity of improvement. Reading and writing, common arithmetic, and the first elements of mathematics, I acquired all of these, but none without some difficulty. My progress could best be described as assured, if not altogether swift. Miss Spencer was a woman of truly bountiful patience who, when I stumbled, always sought to remind me that books are 'fair virtue's advocates and friends', and that reading and writing are procured only by unwearied application, for which, according to Miss Spencer, I possessed a good capacity. She advised me that with a Christian education I would find it possible to behave with reverence to my betters, with civility to my equals, and to subdue in others the prejudice that my colour gives rise to. Soon I came to regret any time that passed away without improvement, and I would employ not less than ten hours of the day in reading.

My uncivilized African demeanour began to fall from my person, as I resolved to conduct myself along lines that would be agreeable to my God. Miss Spencer informed me that good persons, into whose company she would introduce me, minded the Bible. She challenged me to name any bad persons of my circle for whom the Bible was a guide. I could not. It remained for her powerfully to encourage me to drive old Africa clear from my new mind for, as she related, black men were descended from Noah's son Cham, who was damned by God for his disobedience and shamelessness in having relations with his chosen wife aboard the Ark. This wicked act produced the devilish dark Chus, the father of the black and cursed Africans. Miss Spencer convinced me that supplication to God's will would allow me to gain access to the heavenly thereafter, and she described to me the work of the recently successful abolitionists, naturally favouring those with a Christian zeal over the formally humanitarian. Soon after the Lord was pleased to break in upon my soul and cast his bright beams of celestial light into this dark place. Having completed her task, the good angel of Blackheath then set a crown upon my head; banished was black Tom, and newly born she gave to the world, David Henderson.

My master could scarce contain himself in the change occasioned by my residence in Blackheath. He promptly ordered a new livery for myself, and announced a shilling increase in my allowance so that this personal attendant now drew the princely sum of eight shillings a week. Mahogany Nell, who rejected all my efforts to liberate her from her unlettered heathen misery, seemed truly suspicious of my person on account of my new learning and improved bearing. Indeed, a great and lamentable distance grew between us which mercifully tarried on this near-shore of open hostility. Meanwhile Anna, at our master's urging, gave her Christian mind over to perusing several entertaining books calculated for women, in order that she might develop some conversational elegance. Our short courtship produced great happiness on both sides, and I therefore thought it only proper to propose a marriage. Anna, to my barely concealed delight, acquiesced. My master convened an audience with me at which he expounded upon the nature of common opinions pertaining to such a liaison. I confessed that while walking abroad with this female in the Haymarket I had been rudely set upon by a swarm of white *gallants* with epithets of *black devil*, while she that was under my protection received considerably worse for being in company with a man of colour. I set before my master the hope that foul discord might never approach his blessed abode, and promised that my wife and I would withdraw should such a misfortune descend. At this he discerned deeply, which was his custom, before pronouncing, 'David Henderson,' for he was fond of my name, 'your wife and yourself must have shelter beneath my roof, but be ever wary of the disagreeable consequences of such an unnatural connection.' He then continued, and recounted how a goodly proportion of my countrymen had scandalized London society by carrying too far the empire of Cupid. He asked if I had not observed how some of the bawds and lower-class women of England seemed remarkably fond of my complexion. I said that I had, but I pressed on and spoke to him of God's love for all, as long as they be Christian and part of His world. The ill-breeding of the populace concerned Anna and myself only in as far as it threatened our bodily safety and that of our master. We had already supped at the cup of bitterness that would evermore be set before us, and its taste, though unpleasant, had not stricken us a mortal blow. My master stood and paced awhile. He then pronounced that in addition to his permission we should also have his blessing. My heart was over-powered with joy, and his agreement caused me such sensations as I was able to express only in my looks.

Sadly we were soon abandoned, for barely a week after this day our master was hastened to a heavenly world by a sudden squally fever which strengthened in force and blew the life out of his body. My wife and I mourned deeply, and with much volume, but our misery could never compare with the amplitude of the grief displayed by faithful Mahogany Nell. It was eventually considered politic to attend upon her to dam her misery, for we worried that she too might take her leave, but her storm of passion having been unleashed she chose to rail against those closest to her and forcefully bade my wife and I to depart from *her* Pall Mall *mansion*. It was feared (and then confirmed by an attorney) that she in whom no Christian values might be planted would have the good fortune to enjoy the sole benefits of my late master's will. This being the case, my Anna and I were cast out without an asylum of a friend ready or willing to receive and protect us. Mrs Henderson's family were long since scattered and lost, and mine beyond the seas and inhabiting a warmer, but less civilized clime. My raging mind could think only of Miss Spencer of Blackheath as one who might give us tolerable shelter, for my wife and I had nothing between ourselves and the St Giles Poorhouse for Blacks, save only a few trinkets we might offer up to a pawnbroker in the hope of some trifling sum.

Miss Spencer, may the Almighty bless her kind soul, agreed to provide us with temporary lodgings. When we had explained fully to her the nature of our predicament, Miss Spencer declared that the time had arrived for David Henderson to begin his task in life. 'And what task might this be?' I asked of her. She informed me that I must open the ears and eyes of the ruder of her countrymen to the hope of Christian redemption that is buried at the heart of mission work. I alone among my intemperate heathen brethren, who injure their constitutions by too frequent a repetition of the charms of the bottle, might present a spectacle of salvation and collect money for exploratory travels in the country of my birth. That the negro was no longer goods, in the manner of hides, redwood, or grain, had been well-served out by the abolition (although many, including myself, were aware of the unfinished state of this abolition). Miss Spencer insisted that the commonly held assumption that a black Englishman's life consisted of debauchery, domestic knavery, and misdemeanour, served as a false and dangerous model, while the notion of irreversible savagery in old Guinea presented an equally untruthful picture. It was determined that I should tour England as a servant of the Blackheath mission, and in the company of my wife. Upon our return to the capital we would travel to Africa in the office of missionaries and preach the Gospel in the hope of spiritually reforming my former countrymen and persuading them to embrace the faith of Jesus Christ. My exhilaration, on being presented with this solution to the ills that had plagued my life since the departure of my master, was doubled on learning that my stay in Guinea would be brief. Truly I was now an Englishman, albeit a little smudgy of complexion! Africa spoke to me only of a history I had cast aside.

Across the full breadth of fair England we trod, the spectacle of my Christian wife and I sometimes provoking the vulgar to indulge themselves in a banquet of wicked jest. We who are kidnapped from the coast of Africa, and bartered on the shores of America, occupy a superior and free status in England, although an unsatisfactory reluctance to invoke the just English law permits the outward appearance of slavery to be enacted by some persons. This creates in the minds of many true Englishmen a confusion as to the proper standing of the black people in their presence. My divers addresses were often prefaced with exempla of this taxing discrepancy

as I read from contemporary English newspapers on this phenomenon.

*To be sold, a handsome creole wench named HARMONY alias
AMY. Fourteen years of age, she reads but a little. She has a scar
on her breast occasioned by a burn, and a toe cut off each foot. Any
person who may have a mind to the said girl, is desired to apply
before the 30th.*

Such short illustrations seldom failed to produce a gasp of
shame from amongst those present, many of whom secretly
flourished upon bread whose origins lay in slavery. I would
proclaim: 'The air of our island is too pure for slavery to breathe
in!' Furthermore, I would maintain that the maxim, 'Once free
for an hour, free for ever!' should be fervently adhered to. Then
I would quote from the holy book. 'Did not He that made them,
make us; and did not One fashion us in the womb?' This fraction
of scripture was generally followed by a period of contemplative
silence into which I would introduce the notion that such a state
of affairs as exists in England cannot be tolerated under the
government of God. 'Surely,' I would say, 'it is a blasphemy
against His benevolence even to suppose it.' I then continued,
pointing out that the engrossment of the public mind in that
disastrous conflict with France having reached a conclusion,
time and energy must immediately be given over to correcting
the situation of the poor, oppressed, needy, and much-degraded
negroes. Having gained some resigned acceptance of this fact
in the form of nodding of heads and whispered 'amens', I
would then seek to assure my congregation that the painful
circumstances that had forced me from obscurity and set me
before them had not planted in my soul a single seed of revenge
against those who had so cruelly treated myself and my family.
God, I would remind them, is the true avenger of the oppressed,
and that deeply injured race of black men of whom I numbered
but a solitary one would, if supplicated in true humility, always

secure from Him a favourable and candid hearing. Huzza's and tears often followed my delivery, but at this I would raise my hand and remind my congregation that the whole law of God is founded upon love, and the two grand branches of it are: 'Thou shalt love the Lord thy God with all thy heart; and thou shalt love thy neighbour as thyself.' I then swiftly drove home the feathered shaft into their wounded English consciences: 'Again,' I would announce, 'from an English newspaper':

Run away from his Master, a Negro Boy of the Mungola country, named Jamaica. Under five feet high, about fifteen years old, very black features. This Sambo was formerly the property of William Jones, deceased. He is very ill-made, being lame in one leg, stooped in appearance, and Falstaffian in girth; he had when he went away a coarse dark blue linen frock, a thick-set waistcoat, tolerably dirty leather breeches, and set about his head an old velvet jockey cap. A suitable reward will be given to any person who will lodge him in any gaol.

To expose the hypocritical iniquities of English custom was not the main thrust of my mission. Its purpose was two-fold, three fold if one includes the petitioning of the pocket for coppers and shillings, and the thanking of God for feeling and humane hearts and strong natural parts. The first purpose of my mission was to open a school in my native Africa, so that those of complexion might acquaint themselves with knowledge of the Christian religion and the laws of civilization. Those of England, who by means or motives of avarice were dishonouring Christianity, might thereafter witness the unnatural nature of their work being repaired by those of both England and Guinea working together in conjoined brotherhood. It was also intended that those of my native Africa should be given the great advantage of a little learning in reading and writing. Whatever evil intentions and bad motives these insidious robbers might have had, access to the divine goodness displayed in those invaluable books, the Old and New Testaments, ought to be shared with all humanity for the greater glory of our Lord God of Hosts, the God of the Christians!

The second purpose of my mission was to rally support towards the noble purpose of banishing the practice of slavery in the Americas that remain blessed with the good fortune to dwell under the English flag – the jolly Union Jack. I preached that the poorest in England may labour under great hardship, but not one would willingly exchange their status for the life of a West Indian slave. What freeman would resign his liberty for the bondage of the dog or horse? My people are born and sold like animals, tortured and all torn to pieces with moil, hunger, and oppression, and still the haughty English tyrants of the West Indies choose not to hear the loud cries for redress which emanate from the nobler in mind among the English of all classes. I proposed to my audiences widespread days of fasting and mourning for the condition of the West Indian slaves, and days of seeking grace and repentance for the souls of the tropical landlords and owners. I reminded these good people that several ladies in England now refused to drink sugar in their tea because of the cruel injustices done to those employed in the culture of it in the West Indies. I concluded by declaring that sacrifices were demanded of us all, for we were all made in God's image, though some of us be cut in ebony.

The phenomenon of my arrival in distant parts of England, sporting a tinted shade and a fair wife, often occasioned surprise and uproar. My wife and I were accosted in one rooming-house by the master, who had not been present at our arrival. He felt certain that he had seen something black in the form of a man lay hands upon a white woman in the kitchen. Indeed he had, and was much shocked to discover the nature of his error. That I not only resembled a man, but was indeed a part of that host of men created in the name of the Lord, was new education for this fool of weak intellect. His schooling formed part of my mission's purpose. That he was able to observe the fact that I renounced my devilish likeness might possibly have aided other blacks who passed these highways, and prevented their being eventually condemned to London's *bird and beast shops* where, sad to say, negro children are sold for amusement like parrots or monkeys, although the practice of decorating them with gold or silver collars has mercifully fallen from usage. Many of these Englishmen, seemingly unaware that slavery cannot be tolerated in a Christian land, still sought to intimidate black men into obedience, and treated the passing African stranger with unacceptable brutality. It appeared that these *countrymen* had little interest in recognizing or relishing the negro on terms of equality. For my own part, I observed a multitude of household servants in this despised condition, yet there were others whose masters had found occasion to treat them with great decency. One young woman was freshly arrived in Gloucester from her master's Antiguan plantation, and while most were at sea with regard to the sense of her manner of speaking, her master would make a shift to understand her tolerably well. At an inn near Chester my wife and I had the privilege of an invitation to the table of an African merchant travelling with a retinue of his own servants. To my great joy, and to the honour of his nation, he had already embraced the Christian faith. I spoke of my mission and he contributed lavishly with coppers and more. We agreed that our paths should once more endeavour to cross. In conversation he was commonly very pleasant to both my wife and myself, directing us with witty turns and fanciful stories, but never to the prejudice of religion or good manners.

The most despised black man into whose territory I had the misfortune to stray was the notorious fop of Bristol, the improperly named Clarence de Quincy. This minion, spoiled by the indulgence of those for whom he presented a spectacle of novelty, and forgetting that he was a *chance-child* dependent upon the bounty of Christian strangers, assumed airs and spoke loudly of his royal acquaintances amongst the black sons of his native Africa. A boastful man, not given to understatement or modesty of expression, he sought to make a figure that would obscure what he imagined to be the objectionable nature of his complexion, and enable him to occupy the position of general favourite with a reputation for amusing endeavours. His perfumed appearance, made complete only by the ostentatious donning of white gloves, bestowed upon him much renown. This man's vulgar mockery of my Bristol mission made my task, and that of Mrs Henderson, all the more difficult. Proclaiming himself at our first meeting a son of that *over-cooked* race of Adam, this bantam-cock reduced the smaller part of the audience to peals of irreverent laughter with his Drury Lane antics. I prayed hard to my God to forgive this blasphemer.

Winter closed in and my poor wife began to take with fever. Although I was only recently exposed to snow, my Anna seemed to suffer even greater discomforts, added to which she was now happily quite large with child. We sought refuge in a small village in the County of Warwickshire where I discovered, to my despair, none amongst this circle of villagers who appeared to have wholly kept the ten commandments. We were treated with great disdain, and my efforts to preach my chosen gospel fell on deaf ears. My dear wife's condition deteriorated, and she suffered excessively as the winter began to prove remarkably severe. Through lack of nourishment we were reduced to the greatest misery imaginable. My familiar sermon that the mind needs food, as well as the body, was in this instance reversed. But it appeared that we could obtain neither work nor compassion from these people. Being an entire stranger I was shy of making requests in the form of begging, but upon receiving no response to a hastily despatched letter to my Blackheath benefactress I fell into a melancholy repose, thoroughly helpless as to how to act. Reduced to a pitiable state of darkness, possessing neither fire nor candle, and our diet crusts of stale bread and drawn-water, we languished in this condition until my dear Anna's birth pains achieved a regular beat. It was at this emergency that I strode forth, resolved now to make my situation known and throw myself at the mercy of these godless people.

Knocking at the first door that presented itself, I was greeted, kindly and without surprise, by a stranger who was evidently aware of my residence in his village. This good man and his lady wife, gardener and maid, listened in silence to my dismal tale, then accompanied me with bread and ale to the room in which I had abandoned my Anna. But it was to prove too late, for some two hours later my dear Anna Henderson and her newly born child both expired within a breath of each other. My chivalrous friends were concerned at my state of mind, for I keened with grief and would not suffer to be parted from the cold bodies of my beloved family. Many an hour passed before I could be prevailed upon to stand on my own legs. The following day the minister arrived and informed me that my child could not be admitted to the parish soil because he had not been baptized. Furthermore, although I had often spoken fluently and publicly of God, the minister claimed he had no evidence of my own Christian status. At length I informed him that I would bury my wife and child together on common land before I would suffer them scattered into separate graves. This *Christian* man seemed truly amazed at the gravity of my resolve. The bishop of the diocese was sent for and a compromise was achieved whereby the child might be buried with the mother, but the minister would hesitate to read the burial service. To this I agreed, and hoped that by my mien they would understand that I was punishing them with love, for destructive hatred had been driven clear from my heart by Almighty God.

On my return to the great metropolis I was obliged once more to throw myself at the mercy of my great and kind benefactress Miss Spencer, who informed me that she had not been the recipient of my desperate communication. She did respond, however, to the horrors of my tale by providing me with shelter, and nursing my malnourished body into some semblance of health. It was decided upon that my mission ought to go forward, and that although I had exhausted the recently obtained funds on caring for my ailing wife in the County of Warwickshire, the Lord God in His wisdom would certainly bestow His generous benevolence upon me. And so it came to pass, for not a week after we pronounced our resolve to continue with the mission, a messenger-boy arrived with notice for David Henderson to proceed to Gray's Inn and attend upon a Mr Morgan. It appeared that my master's will had indeed allowed provision for his David Henderson and wife Anna, and that the sum of four hundred guineas would soon pass into my possession upon my agreeing to affix my signature to a proffered document. I was one who had, if truth be known, never been able to set a proper value on money, wishing only to be supplied with a small amount to offset immediate necessities. I had determined that whatever capital might exist in surplus was to be given up and used for the greater glory of the Lord. Four hundred guineas seemed an impossible sum for one such as I, and together with Miss Spencer it was agreed that I should utilize this fortune by immediately hoisting sail and furthering my mission on the African coast. It was with great sadness that I was obliged to take leave of my kind patroness and board a ship that was hauling anchor for doubtless ungenerous trade. Miss Spencer gave me many friendly cautions as to how I might conduct myself once back in my unChristian native land, and advised me that I should write frequently. This I promised to do, my heart heavy with sorrow, for it was Miss Spencer who had given me true instruction in the principles of religion and the knowledge of God. We exchanged confessionals of how greatly we anticipated meeting with one another at the close of this very solemn mission.

The captain of our vessel, though clearly unfamiliar with Christian ways, did me the honour of inviting me to share his table for the first week of our voyage. I marvelled at my improved conditions, and related to him the tales of my previous journeys. We toasted in wine the honour due to merry England for having abolished the trade, while other, less civilized, nations continued to pursue this vile commerce. I informed the captain that upon arriving in Guinea I intended to introduce the English system of Christian education. It was God's wish that I should return to my old country with the character of a man in upper rank, and a superior *English* mind, inferior only to the Christian goodness in my heart. My rooming companion, a Frenchman of seemingly noble manner and purpose, proved my only other conversationalist. But to my regret this man, who styled himself an aristocrat, could follow little of my dialogue, and I precious little of his. This proved to be of no true inconvenience to either of us, for we were polite partners.

We were but one day's distance from the coast, when I ventured to retrieve my remaining three hundred and fifty guineas. I was astonished to discover it removed from its hiding place. My first inclination was that the mistake was mine, and so I searched all possible locations. After many hours, and with great regret, I arrived at the conclusion that the wealth of my Gallic companion must have increased during the passage of our voyage. This uncharitable deduction gained credence when I confronted the vagabond. With a flurry of shoulder motions, and gesticulations of the arms, he made it known that I should present my case to the captain. Upon my petition my host and captain ordered his men to throw me into the belly of the vessel and confine me in irons in a condition of captivity all too familiar. The crew brought me water and crusts, but they would not respond to my pleas that the captain be informed that I was willing for he and the French rogue to take my guineas so long as I might have my liberty. My submissions fell on deaf ears, and so my fate appeared to be sealed. I prayed to the Lord that he might spare me, and I made promise that should he do so I would redouble my Christian efforts, for at this moment I very much feared the horrors that lay ahead. My former passage rose in dreadful review and showed only misery, stripes and chains. In one moment of weakness I called upon God's thunderous avenging power to direct the sudden state of death to myself, rather than permit me to become a slave and be passed from the hand of one man to another like a sack of grain. But the Lord, in His mercy, chose to spare me.

We rode at anchor on what I knew to be the coast, for the noises were those of unloading, and the heat and odour that of my native land. In this confined state I made continued and faithful pleas to the Almighty Lord. One whole week transpired before I realized that I would soon be visited by Guinea-men. I heard their voices, shrill in their different native tongues, and then they were upon me and bemoaning the circumstances which had led to their illegal captivity. That I could still make a little sense of my own native language among the many spoken gave me some comfort, but the treachery of these white men, even towards one such as I who esteemed their values, tore at my heart with great passion. That I, a virtual Englishman, was to be treated as base African cargo, caused me such hurtful pain as I was barely able to endure. To lose my dear wife, fair England, and now liberty in such rapid succession! Torrents of tears broke from my eyes, for I knew now that I would have to describe yet another passage of loss. The horrors of this second illegal journey I have chosen to forget, although this unnatural and painful murdering of the memory has caused me distress at least as great as that suffered whilst enduring the voyage. After many weeks of torment, the ship finally came to anchor. Having the advantage of a Christian education, I had no doubt that we were in the region of the Americas. My countrymen, however, were seized with great fear, knowing neither location nor their destiny. We articles of trade, once liberated from the intolerable aroma of the pestilential hold, were directed to remain on deck. From this vantage point we were able to observe the tropical new world that was now, *home*.

The vulgar crew seemed in a state of great joy, knowing that they would soon be on land. I simply listened and fretted at the blasphemous language displayed by these men. Then I caught the eye of both the captain and the Frenchman, but these buccaneers endeavoured to ignore my glare of Christian devotion tinged with anger. Unlike the parishioners of Warwickshire, whom I felt obliged to punish with love, these two devils I would have gladly tossed into the waters. Perhaps they sensed this, for although I made no further application for what was rightfully mine, my gaze provoked much shuffling of their feet. We drew close to the harbour and took cover amongst ships of different sizes and purpose. Under the blanket of darkness many planters and overseers came aboard and divided our black company into smaller parcels before deciding upon their illegal purchases. I faced these white men, with more knowledge of their country than they could possibly imagine, believing that through hard work and faith in the Lord God Almighty, my bondage would soon cease. The African world of my sad, dark brethren had been truly abandoned across the waters. They knew this now. For them a new American life was about to commence.

I alone of my parcel was purchased by a Mr Wilson, who made it known that my title was to be Cambridge. He pointed towards me and repeated the word as though addressing an infant. My visage betrayed no trace of anger. I decided that by degrees I would reveal to them my knowledge of *their* language. Travelling by cart, we passed through the coastal capital of Baytown, and then turned inland. We picked our slow way up a hillside towards the plantation upon which I was to labour as a common slave. I listened as Mr Wilson addressed his black driver. He commented that he believed I possessed more intelligence than the others on offer, which caused me inwardly to smile. However, despite my large frame, he believed my physical strength, while far from disappeared, to be somewhat unsatisfactory when set against the potential lustiness of my fellow cargo. My *master* declared his purchase to be 'calculated'. We arrived at the plantation and I was rudely introduced to a hut which I was led to believe would be my *house*. Once inside I discovered a simple bench littered with straw, and a stench so insupportable that, although greatly desirous of sleep, such a commodity was impossible. I understood, through my own knowledge of the business, that I would be *seasoned* alone. Furthermore, I knew that any sign of indiscipline would be severely punished.

I passed my first weeks in solitude. Only fleeting visits from an exceedingly strange, yet spiritually powerful young girl, who daily brought me food and water, disturbed my isolation. When my seasoning was deemed complete, it was this same girl who began to escort me about the plantation and introduce me to my fellow slaves. My rapid acquisition of *their* language shocked them. I simply explained that I had tarried a while amongst English people, but when pressed I would say no more. I had determined that I would be a strange figure, quiet and reserved, for I intended my residence on this plantation to be brief, and felt that it would be unfair to begin to deliver a *sermon* I might never have the opportunity to conclude. I hoped that none amongst them would take offence at my reluctance to participate fully in their slave lives. Certainly the girl seemed content, and soon I came to develop a true affection for my odd female companion, and she for me. I told the girl nothing of my Anna, not wishing to divulge, in this place of unhappiness, anything of my previous felicity and taint my Anna's memory by association. Young and aloof, my unlikely escort, I quickly discovered, occupied among her slave-peers a position of respect occasioned by a formidable suspicion of her person.

Her history was a sad one. Born on the plantation, her mother had died shortly after her delivery, and her pagan father naturally spurned her. At ten years of age she was *married* to a man twenty years her senior. For three years this man treated her brutally while she *refused* to produce children.

Meanwhile, the evidence of his capable manhood could be seen scampering across the slave village and improving his master's fortune by the minute. Her *husband* was eventually traded to another plantation, presumably to further display his breeding skills, and the girl was once more abandoned with neither protector nor any person who might show her some outward sign of affection. She subsequently developed a sullen nature which caused her fellow slaves to fear her, for their understanding was that the cruelties inflicted upon her during her violent *marriage* had mercly compounded the strangeness that the unloved misery of her early years had forged in her soul.

Now I was manifestly a West Indian slave, but I refused to accept the woeful conclusion that there was little hope of manumission through either the generosity of Mr Wilson, or the evidence of my good deeds. The execrable years bred quickly but never, not for one moment, did I lose faith in the redeeming powers of the Good Lord. My hair took on a grey aspect, and my strength began to fade, yet all the while I remained true to my Lord and hoped one day to be afforded the privilege of preaching again in dear England on the subject of my travels and experiences as a son of God. Sadly, as she budded into womanhood, my strange escort became even more unpopular amongst her fellow-slaves. Her curious mind remained closed, and she seemed incapable of conversing with anybody beyond myself. I talked with her of our Lord, and attempted to explain that Jesus Christ had lain down his life for such as us, but her undeniably spiritual nature was absorbed in an entirely different direction.

The other slaves claimed her to be a possessor of the skills of obeah, but I refused to be drawn into their discussions. I recognized in her a growing aberrance and mind-wandering detachment, yet the loneliness that this *ailment* necessarily bestows upon its victims may have contributed to the powerfully sympathetic affection that I continued to feel towards her. Perhaps we were a case of *curiosity* attracting *curiosity*, for the respect which I commanded on account of my Christian learning and knowledge of the world was matched only by the caution with which every person viewed my woman friend. After a slow and wilfully paced courtship that lasted many West Indian seasons, I, Cambridge the field-hand, requested that the woman occupy my hut as my *wife*. Without uttering a word she willingly agreed, for she was now entering a period of her malady when she insisted that she distrusted words. And so we began to share our lives in my hut, and I watched and cherished her, all the while praying that the infusion of Christian values into her soul might help to obscure the miserable details of her life, which others claimed had resulted in her being *blessed* with this excess of pagan vision.

Years of drudgery lumbered by, and I wondered if I should ever be set free from this unChristian labour. Indeed, I worried that perhaps my God was punishing me for my sinful existence, even though He must have known that should I have requested a Christian wedding ceremony it would have certainly been denied. I had raised the question of my fellow-slaves' continued adherence to crude African religions with our local man of the cloth, Mr Rogers. The minister, whilst openly acknowledging the correctness of my concerns, sought even as he spoke to a black Christian to introduce me to the notion that converted negroes soon became perverse and intractable. He further maintained that conversion was an inadequate tool with which to combat the perpetual absence of the Christian virtues of family life, morality and social discipline that he frequently found in 'the black stock'. Not unnaturally, I felt inclined to ask after him what he therefore imagined his role to be while he existed in this West Indian region, but I desisted, feeling pity and revulsion for this man who would attempt to build a false notion that all of a black skin are tainted with Cain's crime, or that of Noah's son, Ham. This weak man, who without doing a stroke of God's work simply coughed and perspired abnormally in the tropical heat, confirmed my long-held suspicion that many covetous and profligate individuals are often admitted to the clergy. The blocking up of all the inlets to the spiritual regeneration of the negro seemed his sole and devilish task. That such a man might condescend to marry a pair of negroes after the Christian manner was optimism beyond all reason.

One night, on hearing some distant commotion, my *wife* awoke with a start. It was not until the clear light of day that I discovered that the veteran Mr Wilson had been driven off our estate by his overseer, Mr Brown. Mr Wilson had proved himself a tolerably decent man and I, in common with many others, was sorry to see his demise. Doubly so in that he was replaced by Mr Brown, a bullying brute of an overseer who seemed trapped within the imagined swaggering authority of his own skin. His first act was to attempt to reorganize the status among the slaves to suit his own purpose. To this end it was suggested that I accept the title of Head Driver. Not wishing to be master to any, I declined, and so began the period of conflict between myself and this Mr Brown. He could not accept my *disobedience*. Although no words passed through his lips, it was clear that he had determined to reduce the *haughty* Cambridge, who by now had long revealed to all a firmer grasp of the English language than any, including Mr Brown, might ever conceive of achieving. I had also, much to this Mr Brown's chagrin, gained the true respect of my fellow-toilers, who affectionately styled me *the black Christian*.

Life continued without reference to the calendar, until one evening Mr Brown appeared at my hut after dark. His breath was contaminated with liquor and his person evidently consumed with passion. That my poor *wife* was the object of his frothful desire I had no doubt, but I decided that he should not satisfy himself upon her like an animal. As though reading my mind, Mr Brown drew his pistol and ordered me to leave my own hut. The pitiful pleading of my unsound *wife*, who saw that Mr Brown was truly determined to kill me if necessary, encouraged me to leave. Her distress attracted the attention of my fellow-slaves, who stood in the darkness as though this humiliation was something that we ought to endure as a company. Their hidden purpose was clear, for they wished to ensure that I should not decide upon any action, self-destructive or otherwise.

It appeared that my *wife*, in one of her not uncommon flights of fantasy, had recently taken to conducting herself as though the mistress of the Great House. The fearful house-servants were unable to sway her from her queer purpose, and there abounded in the Great House a state of anarchy. However, although my *wife*'s pantomime had been in operation for some weeks, the principal cause of this destructive disorder was not her unseemly behaviour, but Mr Brown's inexplicable toleration of this charade. His *patience* extended as far as allowing her to share his table. Perhaps he looked upon my comely *wife* as a visual entertainment, in the same manner that some Englishmen keep about them dwarfs or pet monkeys? Or was he lonely? Or was he simply humouring her in anticipation of this moment when he might punish both my *wife* and myself with one act of brutal desire? I prayed to the good Lord to release my poor simple *wife*, who, although not my wedded wife in his eyes, meant as much to me as any who might occupy that station. And then my God answered me as a sated Mr Brown reappeared, seemingly unconcerned by the suffering he had inflicted, and oblivious of the gathering of slaves, all of whom viewed this man as a disgrace to his own people and their civilization. The next day Mr Brown found weak pretext to inflict upon me a severe beating in the presence of an English female. Whether this was some customary ritual to ensure easier access next time he should choose to visit my *wife*, or due punishment for the defiance I had chosen not to hide, I could not tell. But upon my back, in a series of random patterns, were markings that cut deep into my flesh.

After Mr Brown's violation the bond between my *wife* and

me, although still intact, began to be tried beyond its strength. The woman steadfastly refused to adopt the Christian religion, which continued to cause some unpleasant friction between us, but to my horror she now reverted to dirt-eating and other abominations. I traced this filthy behaviour to a *sickness* brought on by Mr Brown's hunger, although this by no means justified such paganism. For his part, Mr Brown continued to trifle with her reason by tolerating her fanciful delusions as she continued to sport herself as the mistress. It was, however, the arrival of the English female that seemed to pitch my *wife* into her final and irrevocable madness. This Englishwoman, the daughter of our true owner, appeared amongst us, and after an extended convalescence she entered fully into our miserable society. On the rare evenings when my *wife* paid me the compliment of returning to my hut, she began now openly to mock at my Christian beliefs and to scream out for her long-lost mother. This caused my heart to swell with both sorrow and anger, for, as is well known, a Christian man possesses his wife, and the dutiful wife must obey her Christian husband. Accordingly, at the conclusion of the week's labour, I decided to seek an audience with Mr Brown at which I intended to instruct him to cease indulging my wife's behaviour, and to offer him the opportunity of cleansing his heathen conscience and confessing his role in her recent sad demise.

On a bright Sunday afternoon, when the white people had returned from church, I presented myself beneath the piazza where Mr Brown was taking tea with the Englishwoman, in whom he appeared to have developed an intimate interest. Clearly he knew the subject and object of my visit, but giving me no time to state my purpose he barked rudely that I had no place petitioning him – this ungodly man! – on the Sabbath, and he declared that I should remove myself immediately. I hesitated, and then began to speak, whereupon Mr Brown climbed to his feet and, turning a murderous vermilion, bellowed that I should immediately absent myself. On receiving this instruction I turned and left. I returned to the negro village and sought out my *wife*, who was occupying herself by singing meaningless ditties. I knew now that her mind would stray more frequently into zones of illogicality, for not only would Mr Brown continue to torment her, but her abuses were now compounded by feelings of jealousy. I knew also that come the morning I might reasonably expect to be flogged for my *impertinence*.

To my surprise Mr Brown, while eyeing me unmercifully, chose not to lash me. This was fortuitous for us both, for I had resolved to no longer endure his abuse if applied in the only manner he seemed to understand, in other words, unjustly. I had decided that I would resist, without turning my mind to a heroic mission, for my knowledge of the Bible instructed me that it is man's duty, with God's blessing, to outwit tyranny in whatever form it appears. My battle with this Mr Brown was now couched in terms of a holy crusade which, with the Lord's help, I was determined to wage with all the energy and skill known to me. The Englishwoman did not concern me. She seemed decent, if a trifle over-dressed for the heat, and she adopted a not altogether unsurprising posture of social superiority driven home by the alabaster in her complexion. Seldom without handkerchief to ward off the fetid air, she graced us with a detachment that bordered on thinly disguised disgust. That I might have conversed with her at ease, perhaps even discussed acquaintances in common, undoubtedly never occurred to her. However, Mr Brown's obsession with this woman, and his lack of attention to my *wife*, caused my *wife* further to enter that region of the mind whence all attempts to retrieve her are rendered futile.

Mr Brown frequently made it his business to travel to distant plantations and remain there, sometimes for many days. It was while he was engaged upon one of these journeys that I was called by Stella, the attendant to the white lady, to hurry to the Great House. It appeared that my *wife* had finally done mischief enough to render her presence offensive to all, black and white. Howling in her bizarre manner, scratching at the dirt, and picking lice from her skin, my *wife*'s mind was no longer her own. Labouring under the full weight of public humiliation, and feeling dreadfully spurned, she now considered herself little more than a common animal, and she was acting accordingly. I mounted a guard at the door of the woman, Emily. She was *white* with fear that my *wife* might enter and cause her harm. I assured *the fair one* that she had nothing to fear, and enquired if she were a Christian believer, to which she answered that she was. I asked from which part of fair Albion she originated, and if her father approved of the institution of slavery, to which she replied that she imagined he did, but her attitudes were her own and somewhat different. She declined to share them with me, but seemed truly fascinated by my knowledge and fluency in *her* language, the origins of which I, in turn, declined to share with her. Then our conversation was terminated by the arrival of the doctor, who delivered me a gaze of such contempt that I was obliged to turn from him lest I provoke his humour to an undignified pitch. Stella brought me refreshment, and suggested that I might order my *wife* to cease her noise. This I did, my voice charged with anger. I then departed for my hut.

Clearly my *wife* was beyond my full jurisdiction. After a great number of sleepless nights, in which I asked God not to abandon me in my distress, nor cast me from His mercy for ever, my weak constitution could no longer withstand my shameful torment. The Lord had hitherto shadowed me with the wings of His mercy, and I had great hope that He might appear again for my deliverance. To this end I arose and set out to walk the full distance to Baytown, all the while reflecting upon my eternal state, and determined, before it was too late, to refresh my bond with the Lord with powerful purpose of heart. It was while praying in the *Ebeneezer Chapel* that I finally, with the aid of my merciful redeemer, devised a Christian plan. It was evident that Mr Brown was both the object of my anger, and the cause of my *wife*'s present misery. I would visit him, irrespective of his wrath, and talk to him as one man to another. Upon representing myself I would no longer be swayed from my purposes by either his clamouring voice or his raised fists. That he must cease his tormenting of my *wife* would be the main thrust of my message. I knew full well that a Christian man must fear nothing but the Lord Himself. As I tarried on my knees I felt sure of my purpose. I was determined to carry out my scheme, and then make every exertion to obtain my freedom and return to dear England. In this frame of mind I left the Chapel and began the long walk back to the Great House.

Once there I presented myself in the kitchen, where I informed Stella that I was hungry. She chose to supply me with beef and bread. She was visibly distressed by my troubled countenance, but I imagined her to be somewhat reassured by the signs of my continued moral strength. As I left the Great House a young white overseer challenged me to explain why I was not present in the fields. I informed him of my need for spiritual counsel at this cross-roads of my life, and he scoffed. I then marched purposefully to my hut to study my Bible. I soon discovered that, as ever, my wayward *wife* was not present. However, I turned my mind towards the Lord and prayed for her pagan soul. Later this same day, my body and spirit being refreshed, and my hunger satisfied, I was preparing to take an evening promenade when Mr Brown entered my hut and accosted me. He knocked the holy book from my hand and proceeded to beat me most savagely. He then demanded that I parade myself before him on this same evening, and until then to refrain from contaminating his other slaves with my insolent presence.

I remained in my hut. In the evening I attended upon the hearing where, among other crimes, I was accused of stealing food! Judgement upon my *case* was postponed, and I was confined to the slave village. For many weeks I supplicated myself in isolated meditation. My loneliness and humiliation without my *wife* (who had resorted to the new ploy of running clear away), the injustice of my treatment, and the Christian import of the season, all served to strengthen my resolve once again to challenge this Mr Brown. I made my way to the Great House and enquired after Stella for his whereabouts. A tearful Stella (for it appeared that Mr Brown had taken no interest in her beloved Miss Emily once the details of the latter's condition had been discovered by the physician) informed me that on this festive day the unloved Mr Brown would soon be returning from church.

I went out on the road, and as I saw his bay mare approach I called to Mr Brown and made note of the anger in his eyes. He dismounted and walked towards me with whip raised, but I had steeled myself to endure no further abuse. In a simple and Christian manner I was merely requesting that he behave towards myself and my *wife* with a decency that one would have afforded a dog. He struck me once with his crop, and I took it from him, and in the resultant struggle the life left his body. I then fell to my knees and prayed to my God to forgive me for my wretched condition. I, Olumide, who had become black Tom, then David Henderson, and now Cambridge, had broken one of God's commandments. On this Christian day, and for the first time since my second unChristian passage, I was truly afraid, truly frightened of my actions and the fearful consequences of my heathen behaviour.

I say again: Pardon the liberty I take in unburdening myself with these hasty lines, but the truth as it is understood by David Henderson (known as Cambridge) is all that I have sought to convey. Praise be the Lord! He who 'hath made of one blood all nations of men for to dwell on all the face of the earth'.

III

'In the year 18—, another murder was committed, the details of which are as follows: – A person by the name of Brown was living as an overseer upon an estate called ———, now in the possession of Messrs ——— and ———. The negroes on this property had been for a long time in the habit of pilfering, and in many instances Mr Brown had discovered the pilferers (offenders), which caused him to be disliked, and determined one among them, more heartless, perhaps, than the rest, to undertake his destruction. On Christmas day, the Christian Mr Brown rode to church at ———, and upon his return in the evening, between the hours of six and seven, he met with his untimely death.

The *mature* slave to whom Mr Brown had rendered himself particularly obnoxious was named Cambridge, and this insane man had long lain in wait for an opportunity of completing his crime, and for the purpose had sharpened an old copper skimmer (used in boiling sugar), which he thought would prove an effective weapon.

Mr Brown, like many other white men in this island, carried on an innocent amour with a woman belonging to the property, named Christiania, and it was the first intention of Cambridge to murder her as well as the overseer. It appeared that this Cambridge had for many years held the poor Christiania in bondage, his mind destroyed by fanciful notions of a Christian life of moral and domestic responsibility which he, in common with his fellow slaves, was congenitally unsuited to. When the unfortunate Christiania would not submit to his thraldom, Cambridge cruelly cast her from his hut and vowed that he would one day seek revenge for her *disloyalty*.

On the Christmas day, Cambridge dressed himself in his best suit, and proceeded to the Methodist Chapel at ———, intending upon his return home to this day brutally murder Christiania, who would never choose to darken a place of Christian worship, being fatally addicted to the superstitious belief in witchcraft to which Africans are so prone. In pursuance of his plan, he hurried out of Chapel immediately after service, and hastened back to the estate. After waiting in vain for a long time, a group of jolly negroes at length sauntered by. Cambridge, whose stock of patience was exhausted, joined them, and asked if they knew where Christiania was? In answer to his query they informed him that she was visiting a neighbouring estate. Thus thwarted in his views of obtaining revenge, Cambridge's designs upon Mr Brown gained double hold of him. He returned to his hut, disrobed himself, put on his working-dress, and first telling *his* Good Lord, "That he had lost an opportunity, but he would take good care he did not lose the next," quitted the house, taking the old copper skimmer with him.

It was a beautiful evening; the moon shone in all her splendour, and every star that twinkled in the heavens glittered around that murderer's step. Oh, that such dreadful thoughts should have possessed that man's mind in the midst of such a lovely scene upon the evening of that very day when angels proclaimed "Good will towards man!" But, alas! –

Nor grateful evening mild, nor silent night,
——— nor walk by moon,
Or glittering starlight,

had any effect upon his hardened heart.

His soul was dark within;
He lived but in the sound
Of shamelessness and sin.

Many a minute stole away, and Cambridge (who had concealed himself in a cane-piece, bordering the road his intended victim must necessarily pass) kept his fatal stand. Not a sound was heard, save the evening breeze as it whistled among the long leaves of the sugar-cane, or the occasional croaking of some night reptile. At length, the tread of a horse's foot was near, and warned the murderer to be upon his guard. Unconscious of the dreadful fate hanging over him, the good Mr Brown rode slowly on, accompanied by a faithful black boy, when, as he was passing between two cane-pieces, just where the canes grew thick and high, with one bound the murderer was upon him. A heavy blow from the sharpened skimmer upon his head stunned him; and ere a prayer could rise to his lips, his soul flew to meet his God, and his murderer was left standing alone, with the stain of human blood upon him.*

The boy who accompanied his unfortunate master fell from his donkey; but as he was unperceived by Cambridge, he was enabled to make his escape into the cane-field, where he remained an unknown observer of the dreadful event. As soon as the murderer had quitted the spot, the boy hastened to the overseer's house (not far distant) and related to all the fate of his master, and the name of his destroyer. An immediate alarm was given, and, guided by the boy, they quickly reached the scene of the murder, where they discovered the unfortunate overseer, bereft of life, and presenting an appearance too horrible for description. They then proceeded in quest of Cambridge, whom they found at his hut, with his blood-stained garments still upon him, and in the act of washing his unhallowed hands.

---

* The negroes say that no grass has ever grown in the spot where the blood dropped since the time of the murder.

After a coroner's inquest upon the body, and a verdict (according to the circumstances of the case) returned, the *Christian* Cambridge was conveyed to the capital, where he took his trial for murder. He was found guilty and condemned to suffer death by hanging; and to make the punishment more impressive to others, he was ordered to be carried to _____ Pasture, in the vicinity of the spot where the murder was committed, and there to be hanged and gibbeted.

Long did his whitened bones glisten in the moonbeams; and as the wind shook the chains which held the body, many a little negro who has strayed that way in search of guavas, fled from the spot, for fear of the "dead man's jumby".'

Epilogue

The shallow basin of rose-coloured water stood between them. Emily watched as again Mr McDonald dipped his hands. He allowed the water to run like lace through his fingers. Then he dried his hands purposefully on the silently proffered towel.

'Thank you, Stella.'

The light from the kerosene lamp caught Stella's eyes. Emily could see that they were opaque and distant. For this black woman a terrible ordeal was reaching its conclusion. The man dabbed at his brow and then he was finished. Stella retrieved the sodden and crumpled towel and withdrew herself to a far corner of the room. Mr McDonald eyed her lumbering gait. Then he turned back to face Emily.

'And when will you be returning to our country?'

'Our country?'

'England, of course.'

England. Emily smiled to herself. The doctor delivered the phrase as though this England was a dependable garment that one simply slipped into or out of according to one's whim. Did he not understand that people grow and change? Did he not understand that one day a discovery might be made that this country-garb is no longer of a correct measure? And what then?

It had been a bright clear morning when the doctor arrived. Stella had summoned him. To be more accurate, one of Stella's people, under instruction from Stella, had hastily mounted a mule. He beat the poor exhausted animal the few miles into Baytown in order that he might inform Mr McDonald that Miss Emily's time had come. And so indeed it had, with contractions of monstrous proportions, and a fever that Stella tried to dowse with a dozen dampened cloths. But it was the heat that caused Emily the greatest suffering, the heat and the babbling voices of nature which saluted this day as any other. And then Mr McDonald broke into Emily's half-world of pain and numbness ('Please keep still and stop talking. Stop talking'), and his hands, his large clumsy hands, and Stella like a dark butterfly hovering, silently darting first this way and then that, obeying, concerned, and again Mr McDonald's hands.

It was a distraught Stella who carried the lifeless body of the child clear out of Hawthorn Cottage. It was Stella who rapidly committed the thing to the ground. It was Stella. Darkness fell as she patted the last cake of earth onto the pitiful mound. Then she climbed to her weary legs. Through the unshuttered window Emily could discern the moonlit silhouette of her grief-stricken companion. How Stella had hoped for something they might share. Emily watched as the black woman dried her eyes on the hem of her flour-sack cloth skirt. Then she moved out of sight. Emily listened as Stella walked slowly to the stand-pipe and ran water into a shallow basin so that Mr McDonald, who had recently completed his auscultations and palpitations, might now wash and dry his hands. Emily dreamed of something that she might give Stella to replace that which had been lost. Something that the two of them might share. England?

'I expect I will soon return to England.' Emily paused. 'After all, it is my home.'

'Good, good. Of course.'

Mr McDonald seemed cheered by this news. He carefully pushed the shallow basin to one side with the outside of his polished boot. Then he draped himself about a rocker in the self-satisfied manner of one whose laborious task has come to a successful conclusion.

'I daresay we might even find ourselves as travelling companions.'

Emily changed positions. She hoisted herself upwards by a few degrees. She could now see that the sky held the full shield of the moon, clean and white and pure. And then Stella emerged from the darkness and spirited away the basin.

'Travelling companions?'

Mr McDonald seized his opportunity.

'Your father's decision to sell up means that I find myself well advised to take my leave. I'm afraid that his plantation provides the bulk of my income. Never mind, I'll establish a small country practice, or some such thing. Nasty business a bad crop, especially now. But he should get a fair price for the blacks. Should be a few years before this emancipation thing takes a grip, if it ever does that is.'

Stella re-emerged from the shadows with a fresh pitcher of cold water. She poured some into a glass, noisily ringing the two vessels together. Mr McDonald watched but said nothing further until Stella had once again withdrawn. Emily set down the now empty glass on the bedside table-top. She dabbed at her mouth with a lace handkerchief. She felt weak and empty. Literally empty. She disliked the patronizing tone in the voice of the doctor, as though he had cured her of some terrible ailment.

'I take it you're not an emancipationist.'

Emily ran an idle hand through her hair.

'You may take it that I am not sure of what I am.'

The doctor laughed nervously.

'Your wit reminds me a little of old Wilson. Poor devil's been outdone again. But it's said that he'll stay on as a merchant of some sort. It's doubtful that he'll ever leave these parts. Strange fish.'

Emily lowered her eyes. The silence was peaceful. She no

longer cared for the presence of the doctor. Then, after some awkward creaking of the rocker, the doctor drew himself to his feet.

'I do hope my driver hasn't made off without me.'

Emily said nothing. Stella reappeared and handed the doctor his hat.

'I'm so terribly sorry, Miss Cartwright.'

Mr McDonald bowed sharply. Stella escorted him to the door and waited there until neither she nor Emily could hear his carriage. The night was once more their own. Stella closed the door. Her tasks were complete. All that remained was for her to turn down the lamp and retire to her small room. This she would do, but not before placing her hand on the arm of Miss Emily and giving it a tender squeeze. Emily looked up at Stella. Goodnight my Stella. Goodnight Miss Emily.

Emily lay in bed. She gazed up at the unceiled roof. The dead of night. Stillness. Then she listened as a lizard played beneath her window, tireless, noisy, awkward. Snatches of remembered prayers andanted their way through her head. Emily caught and held one. In a high breathless tone she hurriedly recited it, dedicating the prayer to those, like herself, whose only journeys were uprootings. And now she recalled the day.

'It's doubtful that he'll ever leave these parts. Strange fish.'

Emily lowered her eyes. Something had merely sheltered in her body. She had felt a certain relief at expelling it, covered as it was with a greasy film. Mr McDonald moved her gently to one side and revealed the dark medal of blood which stained where she had lain. Stella had already rescued the carcass. She stood weeping behind the table upon which stood three squads of bottles containing fluids of the unlikeliest colours. Soon Stella would step outside and introduce the child to the earth. Emily would not answer Mr McDonald's gaze. His silence begged her to try and live bravely and put aside any desire to feel a child's mouth on her breast. Put aside any desire to feel a kiss of undoubted devotion and dependence, unlike that of a man, a kiss which might cause a confident radiance to sear through her body. The slave-doctor looked her up and down with great economy of movement. Emily continued to ignore Mr McDonald. She watched the lamp, its orange flame, the clouds of smoke, the soot blackening the roof, and she sunk deeper into indifference, wrapping it around her like an old and friendly blanket. Unpleasant thoughts broke into Emily's bruised mind. They sought to further disfigure her memory. She turned away from Mr McDonald. Her body curled slowly into a protective foetal ball. She remembered her great thirst through pregnancy, her burning desire to taste the milk-stained breath of a child, and then . . . how was it possible for a whole life to vanish before it has begun? How could so much love and care be squandered on the production of a child who selfishly reaches the far side of life without travelling through this one? Like goods in a shop-window, Emily knew she was becoming faded by too many bright mornings. She lifted her hand from her forearm and noticed the light blue finger-bruising against her white skin where she had held herself tightly. Her body had worked spitefully against her, as her mind did now, Go away, Mr McDonald. Emily attempted to console herself with the hope that time would chill the channel of her emotions, and that eventually the incessant waterfall of memory would freeze solid at its source. And then there would be peace.

'I do hope my driver hasn't made off without me.'

Emily said nothing. Stella reappeared and handed the doctor his hat.

'I'm so terribly sorry, Miss Cartwright.'

Mr McDonald bowed sharply.

At the dead of night, Emily climbed from her bed. She stood naked before a mirror that was powdered with the light dust of neglect. She noted (with a resigned sigh) that the masonry had truly tumbled from all corners. She noted that beauty was in the process of abandoning her, that the lined ruins of her face were telling her a story that did not please her. My God, I'm only . . . Emily had aged as pregnant women age. Her face and hips had broadened as one. Her lightness of step had gone as though her foot had been chopped off. Her body had become leaden, but her vision had begun to pulsate with a new and magical life, her mind had become a frieze of sharp stabbing colours. Love, love, love. You see, I'm not such a bad woman am I? Except love for him ran only a short distance. To the point where he was losing control. And freedom. She knew this now. And then it was turned off. And forgotten. A mistake. She fell over like a foal. Emily thought warmly of Stella. Without doubt their greatest virtue was their unswerving loyalty. Dear Papa, your negroes are a deep, oily black, with the occasional matt one dulled by the sun. Emily looked in the mirror at the reflected evidence of her full, idle breasts. They had dropped and now rested heavily against her chest. Below them her belly stood up proud, a house of life which had shamefully pitched out its tenant. Emily turned her head and laughed as she watched moths breaking their wings against the glass chimney of the lamp. Above the stridulation of the crickets she heard voices. She wondered about her child, who knew nobody. Now she must keep it company. Soon. And her travelling companion, Isabella. Poor, good Isabella. They were close, mother and daughter (almost), their words running and racing like rivers, locked together at one moment, the next parting into separate streams of consciousness, then coming together again in a great burst of happiness. Now suffering on the ship. The beads of sweat individually spaced on her brow. Fever began to disfigure her ivory flesh, and then life was snatched from her just when she thought joy might finally present itself in the form of adventure. Her eyes were open, the stare clear and unglazed. Do not (Isabella had reminded her) grow old in a place that is unkind to you. They were kind, they journeyed up the hill and brought her food.

Cassava bread and bush tea mixed with milk. The mistress.
Six months, six weeks, six days, it mattered little for her status
was secure. The mistress, she had a position, but they would
never learn to read and understand her strange moods. And
now fallen upon curious times, standing alone and listening
to the voices that disturbed the night. Papa, was he dead?
His endless pleas for her to return. To Thomas Lockwood?
Papa dead? No. Would she be forgiven for her indiscretion?
There was once a threat of impending arrival transported to
her by a sad Mr Wilson. He could not lift his eyes to meet
the glare in hers. Doomed. She laughed at him. He looked as
though he might shed tears. And then Mr Wilson rode off and
never came again to visit. And Papa's threat was never executed.
And now? Was the pleading at an end? I'm still here. Emily
gestured, palms upturned, eyebrows arched. Are there no ships
that might take me away? But take me away to what and to
whom? She giggled. A man strung up, mouth agape, tongue
protruding. Hercules. Cambridge. With his Bible. Murderer.
A slow chill rippled through her body. ('Please keep still and
stop talking. Stop talking.') To encourage the delicate head
of a child to lie peacefully in the shallow valley between her
fallen breasts. But now now. The head ballooning out of her
body into the earth. Emily squashed a mosquito against her
arm, brushed it to the floor, and wiped away the blood with
the back of her hand. Her autumnal eccentricities. Premature.
Turning the last corner of beauty. Stella claimed that the estate
would be sold off in small plots to free whites and mulattoes
(and negroes who could afford such things). Ah, thought
Emily. Ship? Useless thoughts fell quietly like over-ripe fruit
into freshly lain snow. Snow-white face, unseen snow, never
again. Emily. Miss Emily. Emily Cartwright. Emily. Emily.
Inside of me once. The little foreigner now no longer resident
in my womb. I speak and Isabella answers, and now silence.
Emily listened. In this small cottage she listened carefully but
heard nothing above the noises of the night. Quick, come quick,

death. Emily understood that the patient ones decentre quietly and with more beauty. I have been patient. Quick, come quick. Quick.

Emily stood before the mirror. And now sunrise. She knew that she must bear the weight of yet another day. She knew that she must endure the undignified mêlée of dawn. She knew that, in all likelihood, she would have to witness the dying of the sun come dusk. She understood this. The fragrance of poinsettia came wafting into the room in small eddies that caused the light in the lamp to dance in tune to the scent. She remembered. Journeying up the hill to Hawthorn Cottage. With her friend. Stella. Dear Stella.